BILLY GREEN
SAVES
THE DAY

Ben Guyatt

BILLY GREEN
SAVES
THE DAY

DUNDURN PRESS
TORONTO

Editor: Michael Carroll
Design: Erin Mallory
Printer: Webcom

Library and Archives Canada Cataloguing in Publication
Guyatt, Ben
     Billy Green saves the day : a novel / by Ben Guyatt.

ISBN 978-1-55488-041-6

     I. Title.

PS8613.U927 B45 2009   jC813'.6   C2009-900503-4

1 2 3 4 5   13 12 11   10 09

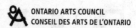

We acknowledge the support of the Canada Council for the Arts and the Ontario Arts Council for our publishing program. We also acknowledge the financial support of the Government of Canada through the Book Publishing Industry Development Program and The Association for the Export of Canadian Books, and the Government of Ontario through the Ontario Book Publishers Tax Credit program, and the Ontario Media Development Corporation.

Care has been taken to trace the ownership of copyright material used in this book. The author and the publisher welcome any information enabling them to rectify any references or credits in subsequent editions.

J. Kirk Howard, President

Printed and bound in Canada.
www.dundurn.com

Dundurn Press	Gazelle Book Services Limited	Dundurn Press
3 Church Street, Suite 500	White Cross Mills	2250 Military Road
Toronto, Ontario, Canada	High Town, Lancaster, England	Tonawanda, NY
M5E 1M2	LA1 4XS	U.S.A. 14150

Mixed Sources
Product group from well-managed forests, controlled sources and recycled wood or fiber
www.fsc.org Cert no. SW-COC-002358
© 1996 Forest Stewardship Council

ANCIENT FOREST ™
FRIENDLY

To my mother, Myrla,
who introduced me to the wonder of history.

PROLOGUE

A light drizzle fell amid cherry blossoms swirling through the humid air. An opulent horse-drawn carriage emerged from the mist as hurried hooves echoed off the cobblestone path. The driver commanded the animal to stop, its heavy breath obscuring its black head.

A sentry holding a lamp stepped forward briskly and offered his trembling hand. "They're waiting for you, sir," he said nervously.

George Clinton, a distinguished man of seventy-three, awkwardly descended with the aid of a cane and slapped the sentry's hand away. *"Well?"* Clinton boomed as he wiped away the moisture from his balding head.

The sentry gawked at him dumbly for an instant, then stepped back and snapped a perfect salute. "Sorry … sorry, sir."

Clinton half-heartedly returned the gesture and limped toward the White House doors. Then he stopped, glanced over his shoulder, and smiled. "Sorry, son." He peered skyward, his eyes flickering against a now-steady rain. "Age, politics, and the sniff of war tend to quicken one's Irish temper." Sighing, he heaved himself up the steps.

The doors swung open to reveal the vivacious, buxom Dolley Madison carrying a sabre. She threw her arms open wide. "Good evening, George. How is the rheumatism?"

Clinton raised a curious eyebrow at the feathered turban she was wearing and hardly stooped to kiss her tender hand. "I daresay my physical pain will be less than my emotional distress after this meeting, Mrs. Madison."

"The wife of the president must always look good," she said proudly, slightly adjusting the turban. "Do you like it? It's the favourite one of my collection. I had it sent all the way from Paris."

"I suppose Napoleon gave you the sword," he said sarcastically, gingerly removing his coat. He handed it to her without looking as she scrambled to set the weapon aside and took the garment.

"If the British are intent upon our demise, I'll be ready for them," she said firmly. "The Boston Massacre, the Tea Party, the Declaration of Independence ... Valley Forge ..." She placed a hand over her heart. "This Quaker girl has seen history in the making."

Clinton rolled his eyes as she grabbed a candelabrum and escorted him to a closed door, their silhouettes dancing eerily against the wall as their shoes creaked heavily against the wooden floor.

Dolley motioned him inside with a toothy smile. "Go on in, George. Everybody's here."

"Thank you, Mrs. Madison," he said, gripping the knob with a gnarled hand.

"Please, George, call me Dolley," she said merrily just as her sword slid away from the wall and clattered noisily to the floor.

"I would prefer not to," Clinton said, shaking his head.

Inside the decorative room Clinton studied the diminutive, sickly-looking James Madison. The president was sitting at his desk, poring over some papers.

Barely raising his eyes, Madison said a bit curtly, "On time as usual I see, George. The door ... please."

Clinton pushed the door closed with an expert flick of his cane before nodding his greeting to the six Cabinet members seated before Madison. Thomas Jefferson, the former president, stood at the window with his back to the room, entranced by the steady rhythm of the rain, his tall, awkward silhouette majestic and somewhat ghostly.

The president got to his feet and motioned to the men. "You know everyone here, George. Please sit down."

"I think I'll stand," Clinton said, shifting his feet. "Just get to the point."

Madison suddenly slammed his fist on the desk, causing everyone to jump except Jefferson, who was still transfixed with the weather. "We've discussed this before! You shall refer to me as Mr. President!"

"Then you will call me *Mr. Vice President*," Clinton insisted.

Both men stared at each other until Madison slid a glass of wine toward Clinton as a peace offering. The vice president waved it off, and Madison walked over to a full-length mirror.

"As you are all aware, with Britain and France at war, the United States has always wanted ... needed to stay neutral," the president said, straightening his jacket before tugging it downward. "I have asked Britain to continue trading with us, but she refuses. She even blockades the seas so we can't trade with France. But perhaps worst of all, gentlemen, many of our ships are being seized and our sailors impressed."

Clinton snorted. "From what I understand most of those seamen are actually British runaways."

Congressman John C. Calhoun leaned forward and casually helped himself to another glass of wine. "I'm more concerned with those Indians led by that heathen Tecumseh," he said with a Southern drawl as he brushed aside his long, thick hair. "He's scaring everybody to death west of the Mississippi."

"You're right, Congressman Calhoun," Clinton said. "It's only *their* land. What right do they have to it? Your wealth has blinded you to reality." He dug into his pocket and flipped some silver at the congressman. The coins fell to the floor, making a sharp noise that echoed in the room. "Maybe that will buy your youth some common sense."

Calhoun scowled. "Pennywise and pound foolish you are. Contrary to what you might believe, none of us need your permission to maintain our struggle against the British for our liberty and independence." He bent down, picked up the change, and deftly manoeuvred one of the coins through his slender fingers. "The only reason you're here is because you *are* the vice president and your support would be ... preferential, shall we say?"

Another congressman, Henry Clay, swallowed the remainder of his drink and greedily held out his glass for more. Calhoun filled it. "And you just know the British are encouraging the Indians to attack us every chance they get. Expanding westward is proving more difficult than we imagined." The man had the whiff of intoxication about him as he resumed shuffling a deck of cards.

"Your insatiable taste for liquor and gambling clouds your judgment," Clinton said to Clay as he moved the wine bottle farther away.

"Would you like a duel?" Clay asked, laughing. Then his fine-featured face grew dark. "I have a well-known temper, Mr. Vice President. You would do well to remember that." He sat back in his chair to reveal a pistol beneath his jacket.

Clinton surveyed the room. "These are all nice speeches, but this isn't the floor of Congress. All you're doing is making excuses for war."

"We're wasting time, gentlemen," Madison said, returning to his desk and unfolding a large piece of paper. "This is a map of Upper and Lower Canada." He reached for an imaginary object above his head. "It is a plum just waiting to be picked."

The others chuckled.

Clinton stabbed the map with his cane. "You're going to throw away twenty-nine years of peace with England for that?" He glared at the assembled men. "The American people won't stand for this!"

Madison resumed sitting and sipped his wine. "Your usual flair for the dramatic has been duly noted ... *Mr. Vice President.*" The president pushed away the tip of Clinton's cane.

"This betrays our own heritage, for God's sake!" Clinton said. "The United States prides itself upon liberty and equality for all ... including our neighbours."

Madison sighed. "Sit down, George."

Clinton shuffled closer to the Cabinet members and looked each one in the eye. "Have you all forgotten how unpopular conscription is?" He glanced at Madison. "And need I also remind you that the debt is already at forty-five million dollars? Pursuing this folly will surely triple that amount! You, Mr. President, will bankrupt the country."

Madison kicked his chair back and pointed a threatening finger at Clinton. "I've had enough of your insubordination in public and in private! You *will* show me my due respect!"

"Men are going to die for the sake of your ego," Clinton said calmly. "You're incubating a lie for the American people. If you truly want war, then attack the harbour in Halifax. That, sir, is where the British navy is based."

Paul Hamilton, the secretary of the navy, cleared his throat nervously. "I ... I must admit we might not be ready for such a conflict."

Madison frowned. "Are you a coward, Mr. Hamilton? You were a professional soldier. I'm sick of your excuses!"

"I just want to be ready, sir," Hamilton said, his plump face flushing.

Clinton smiled knowingly and poured a glass of wine with quaking hands. "You want nothing to do with Halifax because you know the British navy is too strong, not to mention the hundreds of Loyalists who live there."

Madison smirked and admired his reflection in the mirror again. "You *are* jealous of me, George, aren't you? You failed to be elected president twice. That's what's really bothering you, isn't it?"

Clinton clenched his jaw and inched closer to Madison. "I was an unwilling candidate and you know that. The only reason I did run was because so many people didn't want you."

Madison slicked back his snow-white hair. "George, you're nothing but an old, stubborn, unpatriotic man who's lost his will to fight."

Furious, Clinton swiped the desk with his cane and sent the crystal glasses and wine bottle crashing to the floor. "I fought in the French and Indian War!" he thundered as he hobbled to a copy of the U.S. Constitution hanging on the wall. "My name would have been on that document, too, but I was in charge of the militia at the request of George Washington himself. Remember?"

Madison strolled to the crackling fireplace and warmed his hands. "In case *you've* forgotten, I *am* the Father of the Constitution, George. Washington was a good friend of mine, as well, but this is about the economy. Invading Canada is a good bargaining chip against the British."

Congressman Clay aggressively nodded his approval and patted his pistol. "The president is right. Only war will restore America's honour in light of these British transgressions."

"Here, here!" Congressman Calhoun said, pounding the desk to demonstrate his support.

Clinton stared at the Constitution. "War Hawks — every one of you," he whispered before turning to confront the men. "Many of the militias won't even fight outside their own states. New England won't stand for this and neither will Congress. And you, Mr. President, why don't you call this what it really is — Mr. Madison's War?"

The president wheeled to retaliate, but William Eustis, the secretary of war, stood up. "Actually, Mr. Vice President, Upper Canada has many American migrants who are sympathetic to our cause. The entire area is weakly defended and thinly populated, I might add."

Clinton raised his cane and pointed it at Eustis. "Those aren't good enough reasons for spilling innocent blood. As a surgeon, you should know that. Haven't you seen enough killing?"

Eustis ignored Clinton and turned his attention to the president. "Scouting numbers suggest there are fewer than five thousand British troops in North America. Besides, England is too preoccupied with Napoleon to defend such a vast area."

Clinton shuffled over to Madison and placed a hand on his shoulder. "James, please listen to me. I know we've had our differences, but justifying this folly to the citizens of our country will be impossible. Some of their relatives live in Upper Canada, and they'll undoubtedly be caught in the middle. And what about the slaves? They could revolt and side against us. Do you really want to go down in history as the man responsible for such madness?"

Madison slowly removed Clinton's hand. "*Now* you call me James? Go home, George. Go home and let men who love their country do their work."

Clinton searched Madison's eyes for a moment, but the president simply looked away. The vice president leaned closer. "You are a small, small man, James. Maybe that's why you and Napoleon have so much in common."

"Get out!" Madison barked.

Clinton limped toward the door. "The Loyalists are still angry for being robbed of their land and possessions during the Revolution, gentlemen," he said as a burning ember from the hearth leaped to the floor. "If they ally themselves with the Indians, there will be more trouble than you bargained for. I promise you that."

Madison stepped on the ember and crushed it with his shoe. "Perhaps you should join them, George." He gestured at the wisp of smoke curling from beneath his foot.

"How dare you!" Clinton cried, storming toward the president. When the vice president faltered and nearly lost his balance, a few Cabinet members steadied him. "I was a brigadier general in the Revolution! You have no right to speak to me that way!"

Madison smiled thinly. "Maybe it's time for you to retire, George."

An uneasy silence filled the room until Jefferson turned from the window. The aging former president poured a glass of wine. "As the Republican Party founder, I can confidently state that the acquisition of Canada is a mere matter of marching. And that, good sirs, is precisely what I intend to tell Congress." He raised his glass in a toast. "To the annexation of Britain's crown jewel. Let the cannons roar." The men cheerily clinked their glasses as Clinton exited the room.

Surprised by the vice president's sudden appearance, Dolley Madison hid the box of snuff she was using and handed Clinton his cloak. "Good night, George. It was a pleasure to see you again."

Clinton glanced at her sabre leaning against the wall. "I'd sleep with that under my bed if I were you," he said quietly as he closed the White House front doors behind him. The wind was blowing hard now, and a wicked bolt of lightning flashed over the horizon, followed by the crash of thunder. "Fools!" he muttered to himself. "God forgive us!"

CHAPTER ONE

A twig snapped and the young black bear swung its head to locate the noise but soon returned to eating raspberries. The bruin finished gorging and lumbered farther along in search of more food. Pushing through the thick brush, the beast flushed a flock of birds from a small tree. After that everything was silent again. The bear slightly raised its great head to sniff the air. In an instant it turned and reared up on its hind legs. The animal let out a frightening roar, saliva dripping from its mouth.

Billy Green, a teenage lad, stood a few yards away, holding a musket. His piercing brown eyes stared directly at the bear. With a swing of its head, the animal dug at the earth with razor-sharp claws and bellowed again, but Billy stood his ground, his finger slowly wrapping around the trigger.

The beast dropped to all fours and inched closer but suddenly stopped, its eyes locked on Billy's. "I've been following you for almost an hour and you didn't even know," Billy whispered as he reached into a pocket. "I was always downwind. I haven't seen you before. You haven't been away from your mama for long, have you?" He retrieved a piece of beef jerky and held out the meat with steady hands. "Come on, boy, you can have it."

The animal took a few guarded steps and menacingly rolled its head. Letting loose with another blood-chilling roar, the bear returned to its hind feet, mere inches from Billy. The teenager could feel the creature's hot breath against his face as the bear searched his eyes for a sign of aggression or weakness. Then the beast gently took the jerky from Billy's hand and darted off into the thicket.

Billy exhaled deeply and checked his hands. They were beginning to tremble.

"You keep doing that and one of these days you won't be coming home," Adam Green said.

Billy wheeled around to find his father on a ridge, aiming a musket. "Did you see him, Pa? He was beautiful!"

Adam waved at his son to join him on the ridge. "I almost had to kill him, and that would have been your fault."

Billy climbed the steep hill and stood beside Adam, glancing at their farmhouse close by. "I could've shot him, but I knew he wouldn't hurt me."

His father wiped sweat from his brow. "Animals are as unpredictable as people, Billy. And I thought I told you there was work to be done this morning. That flour mill isn't going to run itself. We've got orders to fill."

Billy kicked at some pebbles. "I know but ... but it's boring."

Adam pivoted and placed a hand on his son's shoulder. "Listen, Billy, that boring mill keeps food on the table and a roof over your head for our family. Understand?"

Billy wrapped an arm around his father as they continued walking. "Yes, sir." He studied Adam's leathery face. His father was only fifty, but he looked much older. "You miss New Jersey, don't you, Pa?"

"I miss your mother more," Adam said, looking skyward. "That's why we owe it to her to keep working. She would've wanted it that way."

Billy stopped walking and licked his nervous lips. "Pa ... I want to join the militia."

Adam's face darkened, and he grabbed the musket from Billy's hand. "We've already discussed this and the answer is no!"

"Why?"

Adam hurried into the barn, set the weapons aside, and began piling sacks of flour. "I said the answer is no! Get to work!"

Billy started lugging the bags and stacking them against the wall. "I hear there are soldiers my age fighting on both sides."

"That may be so, but I'm not their father. Let their parents worry about them."

"A lot of people say the Americans could even come here to Stoney Creek and take over this country."

Adam threw the sack in his hands against the wall, causing an explosion of white powder. "It's not going to happen! It's just a stupid rumour." He pointed at his son. "I'm only going to tell you this one more time. There will be no more talk of the war in my house!"

"I'm not a child! I'm a man, Pa!"

"Then start acting like one! No *man* wants war!" Adam snatched one of the muskets. "My brothers were jailed during the Yankee Revolution and one of them died there! This gun doesn't solve anything!"

"Don't you want to fight for your country?"

Adam's eyes flared with rage, but he quickly regained his composure. "I did ... I just backed the wrong side."

"You told me they stole six thousand acres from you in New Jersey because you supported the British. Now you've got three hundred in Canada. What if the Yankees do come here? We have to fight." Billy lowered his head. "And I want to help."

Billy's father sat on one of the stacks and massaged his sore neck. "I've seen war, son. It's not glamorous. It's not exciting. It's bloody and it's something you want to forget but never can."

"You can't stop me ... you just can't!" Billy cried as he ran out of the barn.

"Billy! Billy!" Adam shouted. He tried to catch his son but could only watch as the teenager disappeared into the long grass.

At dawn the distant sounds of birds cooing and the gentle lapping of waves could be heard. Mist rolled in from Lake Ontario, frequently allowing brief glimpses of the smouldering Fort George.

A few seagulls pecked at the sand for food until the boom of a cannon shattered the serenity. Another burst followed and offered a quick flash of brilliant orange from somewhere amid the haze.

"Man your guns!" Brigadier-General John Vincent yelled with an Irish accent as another cannonball whistled overhead and exploded, sparking more fires. "Get the women and children back to the basements! Quickly now!"

The dashing officer assisted a young woman and her child as a flame-engulfed beam fell from the ceiling, narrowly missing them. Then a wall collapsed, catapulting a handful of screaming British soldiers through the air, their clothes ablaze.

Vincent scrambled up a stairway, retrieved his scope, and peered at the lake. Looming on the calm waters, he saw a flotilla of troop carriers headed toward the shore. Swiftly, he turned and spotted one of his officers. "I was wrong! The invasion's coming from the shore! Prepare the men!"

Inside one of the American vessels ammunition handlers withdrew a red-hot cannonball from a furnace and carried it in an iron cradle to the gun. The glowing sphere was rammed inside, followed by the wad. Then the weapon was fired and the process was repeated.

At another cannon a canvas bag was loaded with rocks, metal slugs, and shards of glass. An American officer watched as white and black British soldiers marched on the beach. "Send them the grapeshot!" he commanded as the bag was stuffed into the cannon. "Fire when ready!"

The grapeshot sprayed the British infantry, cutting, slicing, and detaching limbs. Blood-curdling screams pierced the mist. The Americans hurriedly disembarked from their small boats and waded ashore as more ordnance bombarded Fort George.

"This is your chance, boys!" a British officer with a Scottish accent screamed as his troops ran to meet the enemy. "After two bloody days of those Yanks shelling us, it's time to get even!"

The British regulars and militiamen splashed into the water and bayoneted several Americans, but they were quickly overwhelmed. The melee turned the water a cloudy red while men from both armies fought hand-to-hand as bayonets cracked bone and musket balls pierced flesh. Outnumbered, the remaining British hastily retreated, some dragging their wounded comrades beside them.

Vincent watched in horror as a thirteen-year-old British soldier was stabbed in the chest and cried for his mother. A few survivors pleaded for help as some drowned in the shallow water. He scanned the dead and dying on the beach before spying thousands of American troops appearing through the smoke and mist.

"I thought we could hold it," he whispered sadly to himself, sinking to the floor. "I thought they'd attack from across the river." His glazed stare focused on the British flag flapping in the breeze. Oblivious to the burning fort and terrorized inhabitants, Vincent closed his eyes, trying to block out the screams of men, women, and children and the constant racket of cannons and muskets. He trembled uncontrollably and gritted his teeth while beads of sweat rolled off his forehead. Then he jumped to his feet with new resolve.

"Get word to Colonel Harvey! Sound the retreat! Abandon the fort! Burn the munitions and spike the guns! Do it now! We haven't much time!" He looked through his scope again, training the lens on Winder and

Chandler, the two American generals. They were proudly stepping ashore, wearing black cocked hats with gold epaulettes on their coats with silver stars. "We'll meet again, gentlemen," Vincent muttered, collapsing his eye-piece with an expert slap of his hand before running off.

Sarah Foote, a fresh-faced young teen with blond hair, meandered along a well-worn path leading from her small wooden house. She struggled through some bushes into a clearing and then began to run, her heart pounding, lungs burning. Dry knee-high grass crackled beneath her feet, and she began to slow her pace until she finally halted.

Breathless, Sarah closed her deep blue eyes and sat on a fallen tree. She listened to her heavy breathing and fanned herself with one hand before opening the locket around her neck. Sarah studied the strands of brown hair inside and closed it again upon hearing an owl.

A forced smile broke across her face as hands covered her eyes from behind. "I knew it was you," she said as Billy Green plopped beside her. "Owls don't hoot in the middle of the day."

Billy stared at her and edged closer, his lips pursed, but Sarah playfully pushed him off the log. Then she darted away, carrying the hem of her dress as Billy gave chase. "A suitor should court me properly," she said, laughing.

Pursuing her through the meadow and around some trees, Billy gently tackled her to the ground. They engaged in a soft kiss beneath the heavy canopy of foliage before he leaned on one elbow and caressed her face. "We need to talk."

Sarah sat up, obviously troubled. "I can't stay long. I have chores to do."

Annoyed, Billy gathered some stones and threw them aimlessly. "You deserve a life of your own ... away from your father and his beliefs."

"He needs me."

"I need you, too. It's been two years, Sarah. I didn't even know my mother."

Sarah fingered the locket around her neck. "You don't understand. I can still hear her screams ... see her lying there."

Unnerved, Billy put his arm around her. "I know it must have been horrible."

Sarah bolted to her feet. "You don't know! I watched her die!"

"Sarah!" a man's voice shouted.

Billy and Sarah quickly turned to discover Samuel Foote standing a few yards away with a pistol in his hand. The stern face and dark eyes of Sarah's father sent a chill down Billy's spine.

"I want you home right now!" Sarah immediately complied and rushed toward her father. "I told you to stay away from her, Green!"

"She's not a child," Billy retorted.

Samuel raised his gun and pointed it at Billy. "One less Loyalist urchin will make the invasion that much easier!"

Sarah lunged forward and tried to wrestle the weapon away from her father, but he pushed her aside.

Billy advanced toward Foote. "Those threats might work in America, but not here! Like it or not, Canada isn't part of the United States and never will be!"

Sarah stepped between them and tugged at Billy's arm. "Billy please ... don't."

"It's men like you that forced my father to leave New Jersey!" Billy cried.

Samuel moved closer. "Traitor!"

Billy waited, every muscle taut with anticipation as Samuel fired over his head.

"Next time you won't be so lucky!" Foote gripped his daughter's arm and escorted her away as she strained to look back at Billy.

Billy watched them for a few seconds before following a trail to the edge of the Niagara escarpment. He sat on the ground with his feet dangling over the precipice and stared at the tranquil, sparkling water of Lake Ontario. Suddenly, his eyes caught movement below on a ridge. There were flashes of colour through the greenery and the noise of breaking branches. It was a line of British redcoats. He gaped in amazement before scuttling to his feet.

"I don't believe it!" he whispered excitedly.

Billy descended the ridge but froze when several of the flanking soldiers took aim at him. He flung his hands up in surrender. "My name's Billy Green. I'm from Stoney Creek."

Satisfied, the men lowered their weapons and resumed their painful march as Billy kept pace with the column. He studied the dozen beleaguered warriors, their faces dirty and bloodied from battle. A few lagged behind. Some limped, while others were aided by crutches and fellow soldiers. All were exhausted.

"Where are you going?" Billy asked.

"Burlington Heights," one of the men mumbled.

"Where was the battle?"

"Fort George has been captured," one of the men said dully. He had a bloodstained patch over one eye.

Billy grinned enthusiastically. "What was the fight like?"

"Don't ask such a stupid question," the soldier replied in disgust.

Taken aback, Billy slowed. "I ... I want to fight, too."

Another soldier shoved Billy aside, causing him to fall into the mud. "The British Army doesn't need or want the useless militia," the man growled. "Go back to your mother!" Several of the other soldiers laughed as they continued on their way.

Humiliated, Billy wiped the dirt from his face and watched as the platoon plodded out of sight.

CHAPTER TWO

A lamp illuminated the face of a dead young British soldier; his eyes wide, mouth agape. Two American infantrymen picked up the body and lowered it into a trench alongside other fallen redcoats. Dirt was shovelled over the mass grave.

The battle at Fort George was long and bloody, evidenced by the smoke still drifting from the battlefield and billowing in the decimated compound. Mangled bodies were strewn everywhere — British, American, black, and Native. Inside the fort the Yankee forces supped boisterously, huddled around countless campfires outside their tents. Above the fort, in makeshift headquarters, U.S. Generals John Chandler and William Winder relaxed before a roaring fireplace.

"I've had court cases tougher than this battle, John," Winder declared, slightly inebriated as he slurped directly from a bottle of rum. The stout, ruddy-faced officer laughed stupidly and handed the alcohol to Chandler.

"Your love of drink is exaggerating your confidence," Chandler said, preferring to pour the libation into a glass.

Winder grinned. "The British are going back to Burlington Heights to lick their wounds like the dogs they are." He chuckled, kicked off his boots, and plunked his feet on the table. "I'll wager you they give up on the defence of Upper Canada altogether. We've already captured Fort York and burned it to the ground. Their supply lines are virtually cut off." Winder reached for the bottle clumsily and raised it. "We'll march and sail unabated to Kingston, we'll control the St. Lawrence, and we'll strangle the British navy."

"We don't control Lakes Ontario and Erie yet, my drunken friend," Chandler cautioned, corking the bottle.

Winder smiled, closed his eyes, and leaned back in his chair. "Just think of it, our names will be written in the annals of history. It will tell of how we courageously and brilliantly captured an entire country."

He uncorked the liquor again, then staggered to his feet to fill his colleague's glass but spilled it. The rum spread quickly and soaked Chandler's shirt. Winder pretended to have shot him, and they both laughed heartily until there was a knock at the door. "In!" Winder bellowed.

A junior officer entered and saluted. "Sir, I have the final figures."

Impatient, Winder waved for him to continue.

The junior officer read from a sheet of paper. "We had thirty-nine killed and one hundred and eleven wounded."

"Brave boys," Winder muttered, visibly shaken.

"And the enemy?" Chandler asked.

"Fifty-two killed, forty-four wounded, and two hundred and sixty-two captured," the officer said, folding the paper.

"All of them ... on both sides were brave boys," Chandler said, raising his glass and drinking, much to the chagrin of Winder.

"Bring one of the prisoners in here!" Winder commanded, pulling on his boots. The officer disappeared for a moment as Winder buttoned his uniform jacket.

"What are you doing?" Chandler asked nervously.

"I can end this war even faster," Winder said as a scared young British soldier was hauled into the room. "Sit down," Winder ordered, motioning to a chair. The trembling teen took a seat, and Chandler offered him the bottle, but Winder swiped it away, smashing it to the floor. "How many forces do you have at Burlington Heights?" Winder demanded.

"I ... I don't know, sir."

In an instant Winder withdrew his sword and held it to the boy's throat.

Chandler looked on, thoroughly alarmed.

"I don't ... I don't know," the lad said, fighting back tears.

"Liar! I swear to God I'll run you through!" Winder said, pushing the sword harder and causing the skin to break as a tiny line of blood trickled. Beneath the soldier's chair a growing pool of urine began to puddle.

"Perhaps the prisoner can recollect if he has food in his stomach and his body has slept," Chandler said, gently pulling the sword away. He smiled warmly at the young man before gesturing to the American officer to lead him away.

Once they were gone, Winder slammed the door and wheeled toward Chandler. "You should have filled him with buckshot!"

"Prisoners require fair treatment, William! As a lawyer, you should be familiar with that concept!" Chandler yanked the sword away from him. "We're all tired. I know what the stress of war can do to all of us."

Winder collapsed into his chair again, drank loudly from the bottle, and wiped his mouth with his sleeve. Full of disdain, he eyed Chandler from head to toe. "You don't belong here."

"And you do?"

Winder broke into an evil simper. "Look at you. You're a tavern keeper. Once penniless and illiterate, I might add." He drained the bottle, burped, and waved the container in Chandler's face. "Serving up liquor is all you're good for."

"Not all of us were born with a silver spoon in our mouth. But if you'd like, I'd be happy to tell our commanding officer about your treatment of the enemy."

Winder snickered. "Ah, yes, General Dearborn. If it weren't for him lending you four hundred dollars to buy your two hundred acres, you'd still be begging in the streets of Maine. You got rich because of that old man. It's nice to have friends in high places, isn't it?"

"You should know," Chandler said, marching for the door, which opened before he got there.

Haggard and ill, General Dearborn limped inside. Winder and Chandler immediately stood at attention and saluted. The sixtyish officer coughed and patted his forehead with a cloth. "Gentlemen, I have your orders." He wheezed and handed Chandler a piece of paper. Dearborn spied the empty liquor bottle and watched as Winder tilted. "General Chandler, you'll be in charge. I'm too sick to join you." He coughed hard again. "I suggest you sober up, gentlemen, and get some rest. You're going to need it." Slowly, Dearborn turned for the door as Winder and Chandler saluted.

After Dearborn was gone, Winder chuckled and slapped Chandler on the back. "High places, eh?"

The modest Green homestead basked in the glow of a full moon, and the sound of crickets filled the night air, along with the frequent call of an owl. Adam Green stepped onto the porch, lit his pipe, and relaxed into a rocking chair. Levi Green, Billy's twenty-five-year-old brother, soon appeared with their brother-in-law, Isaac Corman.

"Thanks for dinner, Adam," Isaac said, leaning against the wooden railing.

"It was Keziah's cooking, not mine," Adam said, rubbing his stomach.

"I'm not so sure you should thank my father, Isaac," Levi said, slapping his brother-in-law in the gut. "It's his daughter who's fattening you up." The two of them playfully exchanged punches, and Isaac put him in a headlock.

"You're not exactly starving yourself," Isaac said, poking Levi in the stomach.

Billy strolled onto the porch and sat on the steps, lost in thought.

Isaac leaned over and felt Billy's arm. "You could use a little more meat on your bones, boy."

Billy pushed Isaac's hand away. "I'm not a boy!"

Mocking Billy's attitude, Isaac said in a high voice, "All right, *sir*, I surrender."

Levi laughed.

"Shut your mouth!" Billy snapped at his brother.

"Mind your tongue, Billy," Adam said sternly. "We don't speak like that around here. Apologize."

"Sorry," Billy mumbled.

"You hardly touched your supper," Isaac said, lightly tapping Billy with his foot. "Your sister's cooking isn't that bad, is it?"

Levi grinned, pretending to shoot a musket. "He's just mad because he can't fight the Americans."

"That's enough out of you, too," Adam said sharply to Levi.

Isaac rolled up his sleeve. "Let me tell you something, Billy. War isn't what you want it to be. When I fought at Queenston Heights, well, let's just say I saw men die horrible deaths." He pointed at an awful scar. "This is what a bayonet can do to a man."

Billy jumped to his feet. "Do you always have to show me that stupid scar? You've had your turn! This war will be over by the time I see any action!"

Adam stared hard at his younger son. "Watch your tongue! I'm not going to tell you again. Understand?" Billy lowered his head as Adam leaned forward in the chair. "Let's get something straight, Billy. You're not going to fight. That's the way it is and that's the way it's going to stay. This family has suffered enough at the hands of the Americans."

Billy paced the porch. "You can't have it both ways, Pa. You despise them, but you won't let me fight!"

"The subject is closed," Adam said, and began rocking again.

Slapping one of the beams holding up the roof of the porch, Billy said, "You're the one who's always telling me how your brother died and how the Yanks stole your land. I want to join the army!"

"Maybe I shouldn't have told you all those things. It was wrong ... I guess. But this much I do know, you're not going to be in this war." Adam relit his pipe as his eyes drifted off. "I made a promise to your mother. I took an oath on her deathbed that you would be free from the horrors of war, and I intend to keep my word."

"I'm so tired of being babied by you. It's well within my rights to fight the enemy, for God's sake!"

Adam leaped from the chair and gripped Billy by the collar. He pushed his son to the wall and lifted him off his feet as Levi and Isaac tried to pull him off. "You will not take the Lord's name in vain again. Your mother died from years of child-bearing. You owe it to her to stay alive."

Billy wrestled free and gasped for air. "She was your wife. You want me to pay a debt I have nothing to do with. I didn't ask to be born!"

The last comment crushed Adam, and he slowly sank into the chair as Isaac and Levi looked away uneasily.

"I'm ... I'm sorry, Pa. I didn't mean that."

"Are you still seeing Sarah?" Adam asked after a long silence.

"Yes ..." Billy shuffled his feet. "I ... I love her."

"I forbid you to see that girl."

"My personal life's none of your business."

Adam slammed his fist against the chair's arm, causing it to splinter. "She's the daughter of an American sympathizer, Billy!"

"What about you? *You're* an American!"

"I *was* an American, but I'm not anymore. It's bad enough I had to beg the Crown for this three hundred acres of useless land, but to have to endure the likes of her and her father as neighbours — that's unbearable!" Adam got up and started for the door.

"I'm going to marry her whether you like it or not!" Billy cried, scrambling off the porch.

"You do and I'll disown you!" Adam shouted.

Suddenly, Billy halted and turned toward his father. "Then find another son." After that he disappeared into the darkness.

There was an uncomfortable quiet until Adam glanced at Levi. "I want you to stay over and keep an eye on Billy for a few days. If the Americans get this far, Billy's liable to do something stupid."

"I ... I got my own family to look after, Pa."

"This *is* your family," Adam growled. "Just do it." He went back into the house, slamming the door behind him.

At Burlington Heights, situated between the lake on one side and a marsh on the other, the British Army had turned a farm into a fortress. Earthworks were built and eleven guns were stationed behind them. The fields were cleared, trees were felled, and fences were broken to provide a clear firing range should the Americans attack.

Inside a marquee tent, General Vincent sat at a desk with his head in his hands, staring at a piece of paper reviewing the numbers and names of the men killed, wounded, and captured at Fort George. He shoved the papers away, dipped a quill into an ink jar, and scribbled: "This position, though strong for any large body, is far too extensive for me to hope to make any successful stand against superior force understood to be advancing against me."

Vincent closed his private journal, retrieved a fresh piece of paper, and began to write his last will and testament, but stopped when there was a disturbance outside the tent. It burst open as a bedraggled, unshaven man in his late forties barged past the sentries.

"Vincent!" Richard Beasley shouted as the general quickly hid his journal. "These are the damages I expect the Crown to pay for." The man withdrew a crumpled piece of paper and slapped it on the desk. "You've done so much damage here to my farm that you're driving me into the poorhouse."

Vincent sat back and rubbed his bloodshot eyes. "There is a war on, sir, and we need all the help we can get."

"At my expense! Your army has taken most of my crops and livestock. Well, let me tell you something, General, I ain't going to provision you no more because I don't trust you. I don't trust anybody's army. I even heard the Yanks wrecked a tavern down by the lake and stole all the goods. It don't matter which army comes around — you're all a bunch of crooks!"

"Your point is well taken," Vincent said wearily.

"And I'm not the only one, you know. Most of the families around here are driving their livestock into the woods and hiding their valuables." Beasley leaned closer to the general. "So what are you going to do about it?"

The general vaulted to his feet, secured Beasley by the neck, and dragged him to the tent flap. "Take a good look!"

Reluctantly, Beasley surveyed the grim situation — an organized military city of injured and dying soldiers with refugees in tents scattered across the fields.

"I only have eighteen hundred men left, and I'm running out of ammunition," Vincent muttered. "I couldn't even spare the artillery to mark the king's birthday." The general released Beasley, then presented a map to him. "Upper and Lower Canada are about to be captured, and all you can do is whine about your business losses." Vincent threw the damage estimate at the shamed man. "I suggest you take up arms to defend your family and property. Now get out!"

Beasley fled the tent as Colonel Harvey entered. The slim, young officer with jet-black hair watched his superior gaze outside again.

"The war is lost," Vincent announced grimly.

Harvey eyed the map on the desk. "Sir, if I may, the Indians have more to lose than anybody. They won't give up without a fight, and neither should we."

Vincent rested his head against one of the tent poles. "John, we're surrounded and outnumbered. "Do you want more of these young men to die?"

"You're our last hope ... the country's last hope."

41

"I've made my decision. We have to surrender. Now please leave." The general went back to his desk and picked up his will.

Harvey turned to exit but hesitated. "Permission to speak frankly, sir."

Vincent nodded.

"Do you think you're the only one in this?" he asked, causing the general to look up. Nervous, Harvey continued. "Everyone's equal. There's nothing more I'd like than to be back with my Elizabeth, but this is more important. I believe God is on our side."

"You're the son of a clergyman, so it's not surprising you'd say that. Besides, I don't think God takes anybody's side in a war. He would just be disgusted at what men do to each other."

"Well, before you do anything, sir, I think you should ask yourself how you would like to be remembered in history. The future of a nation hinges on your decision." Harvey saluted.

Vincent returned the salute. "You're a talented, hard-working officer, John, but you don't know when you're beaten."

"We shouldn't be intimidated, sir. You've fought in Denmark and the West Indies, and I've seen action in Europe, Asia, and Africa." Harvey gestured outside. "You have men out there who are aching to get even for what happened to them at Fort George. They won't let you down." Harvey waited for a response, but the general just stared into space, so the colonel made his exit quietly.

Vincent resumed writing his will, but suddenly stopped and took a stroll outside his tent. The general watched as the black regiment practised marching under their leader, Captain Robert Runchey. He saw the green-coated Glengarrys, known as the Green Tigers, from the St. Lawrence River, and the infantrymen from Newfoundland, who had left the Rock to escape its poverty, but more important, to help their Mother Country in its fight with the Yankees. There were militiamen from different parts of the British North American colonies, men who had left their homes and family to serve. Finally, Vincent surveyed the numerous Indians, camped according to their tribes, but all working together for a common purpose — to drive the Americans out of their land.

"By God, if it's a fight those Yanks want, then we'll give it to them," Vincent whispered, returning to his tent. He grabbed his will, balled the paper, and tossed it into a nearby fire where it quickly curled and turned to ash.

A lantern swinging from one hand, Billy made his way through the bush, a musket in his other hand. As he approached the edge of the escarpment, he glanced at the indigo sky brimming with stars whose brilliance shimmered off the lake below. His eyes followed the shoreline and spotted numerous fires burning miles apart. "British beacons of retreat," he whispered sadly.

Suddenly, a branch snapped behind Billy, and he doused the lamp. Turning quickly, he discovered six silhouetted men on horseback descending upon him. Billy dropped the lantern and fled into the bushes. *Americans!* he thought, darting through the thick evergreens, feet scrambling over the uneven earth as the sound of galloping horses came ever closer.

When he dropped his musket, he fell to all fours and searched frantically for it. Finding it, Billy continued to bull his way through the thickets, thorns ripping his clothes and tearing his flesh. When he came to a rock outcropping, he slipped behind it and laboured to catch his breath. Blinking, he scanned the murky blackness for movement, his ears picking up the creaking of tree branches caused by the gusting wind.

Mustering courage, Billy stood slowly as an arrow pierced the stump beside him. Out of the shadows, a half-dozen Six Nations warriors materialized with muskets and bows poised. "My ... my name's Billy Green.

I'm a Loyalist. A militiaman!"

One of the Natives stepped forward and offered his hand. "I am Major John Norton, a chief of the Mohawks." The muscular man assisted Billy to his feet. "A true militiaman would not have allowed so many to surprise him."

Embarrassed, Billy dusted off his britches. "I was watching for the enemy." Then he narrowed his eyes. "If you're an Indian, how come you speak English so good?"

Norton smiled. "My mother was Scottish, but my father was Cherokee. We have to fight to preserve our heritage." He gestured at his colleagues.

"I wish I could fight," Billy said as Norton pushed Billy's musket aside. Embarrassed, Billy realized his carelessness and grinned stupidly. "All I get to do is work for my father and ... and dream, I guess."

"You should be thankful," Norton said.

"That's what my pa says."

"He sounds like a wise man. You should listen to him."

Billy shifted uncomfortably on his feet and glanced at the chief. "Can I ask you something?"

"Go ahead."

Avoiding eye contact, Billy said, "A lot of people — not me, though — are saying the Indians will fight for whichever side is winning. They say we're starting to lose this war and that you and your kind will turn on us."

Norton took a few moments to contemplate his answer, then motioned at his compatriots. "As you can see, we of the Six Nations are made up of different tribes. The truth is, all of this land once belonged to us, including adjacent land in the United States. I have no doubt that one day we will lose most of it to the white man because we can't stop their advance. The best we can hope for is that we are treated fairly in our own land."

"But which side has treated you better so far?"

Norton chuckled. "For such a young man you have very political questions on your mind. We don't fight for the British. We fight to keep what we have. Many men from both countries have made us promises. England has kept her word more often. But the winds of change can happen quickly."

"Does that mean you might fight us someday ... fight me?"

"If your generation keeps its word and is as intelligent as you are, that will never happen. Put yourself in our position. What if we took your home and lands and then someone else came along and tried to take what you still had left and what you had lost in the first place? There are some who will fight for the side that will give the most of what was theirs to start with, no matter who it is."

"So it's true. You could change sides."

"One must live in the present. It's our belief the

British will help us the most, and I intend to remain their ally. I gave them my word, and a man's word is his soul and his conscience. The best we can hope for is that the British value their word as much as we do."

Just then a pistol was fired, and everyone wheeled around to discover Samuel Foote standing at the top of a low hill, a gun in each hand.

"Drop your weapons!" Foote ordered. Reluctantly, the Natives complied after Norton nodded at them. Foote drew nearer. "You're trespassing on my land. As for you, Green, if I catch you one more time with my daughter, I'll put a bullet through your skull!"

"You know him?" Norton asked Billy without taking his eyes off Foote.

"His name's Samuel Foote," Billy said. "He moved here from the United States after his wife was killed."

"Murdered!" Foote cried. "After she was murdered by animals like you! I watched her die with a knife in her back trying to run away. Someday we'll kill all of you for good."

"I know the truth, Mr. Foote!" Billy said. "Sarah told me. You built a home and had a farm on land that didn't belong to you. You stole it from the Indians, and a bunch of you killed their women and children first. If I were them, I'd have done the same thing."

"Indian lover! I should kill you right now!"

Before Foote could do anything more, one of the

tribesmen swept up beside him, withdrew a knife, and held it to the white man's throat, forcing him to drop the guns.

Billy held up his hands. "Please! Don't kill him!" He turned to Norton. "Citizens of the enemy must be spared!"

Norton pondered Billy's plea, then gestured for Foote's release. The tribesman set the angry man free and confiscated his pistols. "You're an honourable man, Billy Green," Norton said, slapping him on the back.

Humiliated, Foote scuttled up the hill. "I'll kill you! I'll kill all of you!"

Norton climbed onto his horse. "Now you know how hard it is to love and hate at the same time. Maybe now you understand us a little better."

"I do, but I don't hate Mr. Foote," Billy said. "I think ... I guess I understand how he feels."

Norton smiled. "Perhaps you should tell him that. I wish someone had taken the time to understand at the beginning of this war. Who knows? We might not have had to fight it. Good luck to you, Billy Green." Then he and the other Natives rode away.

"Good luck to you, too," Billy whispered. "I hope we keep our word." He watched as the band faded into the night, his mind replete with lessons learned and words to contemplate.

CHAPTER THREE

The sun peeking over the horizon eclipsed the lingering black of night, streaking the sky with fluorescent crimson. The Foote farm was veiled in mist, the grass moist with dew. The only sounds came from a few morning birds.

Billy stepped out of the low, rolling fog and frantically looked in all directions. Then he ran across a small field leading to the house and crouched. Peering through a window, he spied Foote sleeping, a musket by his bedside.

Quickly, Billy moved along the porch to another window and glanced inside to discover that Sarah wasn't in her bed. He smiled and ran to the barn. Once inside, he climbed the wooden ladder and heard a cow anxiously shuffle its feet. In the hayloft Billy gazed lovingly at Sarah, who was sleeping on a bed of straw. Suddenly aware of his presence, she sat up and rubbed her eyes. "What are you doing here?"

Excited, Billy started to say something but promptly stopped and glanced away. "You like to sleep in the barn ... when ... when you can't sleep in the house, don't you?"

Confused and still dazed, she nodded. "Why are you here?"

"I ... I love you, Sarah. You know that. And I think, well, I think you love me, too, right?"

"Yes. You know I do."

Billy stared at the floor and took a deep breath. "I think we should get married."

"What?"

Billy knelt beside her and stroked her hair. "Let's elope! Tonight!" He quickly fashioned a ring from a piece of straw and pushed it onto her finger. "Sarah Foote, will you marry me?"

Sarah smiled and embraced him.

He kissed her forehead. "I know we're young and our parents will say no. But we have to wait, anyway, until after the war, of course. I'm going to join the army."

Sarah backed away, a sombre look on her face. "I can't have my future husband fighting in some far-off place while I sit at home and worry."

"Are you asking me to choose between you and the army?"

Sarah felt the straw ring. "Yes."

"Why can't I have both? My love for you is as great as that for my country."

Sarah raised herself. "It's not the same."

"But you know how much the army means to me."

He reached for her, but she shrank away. "Apparently, the army is more important than I am." She started down the ladder.

"I have to fight!"

"Why? It's a stupid war. Who cares if we're under British or American control?"

"I do, and so does your father, and mine," he said, following her down.

Saddened, Sarah removed the makeshift ring and gave it to him. "You're right. Our marriage would never be accepted ... by either family."

Billy grasped her hands. "Are you saying we'll never be together?"

Suddenly, the silence was broken by the sound of approaching horses.

Outside, Adam Green steered his wagon toward the Foote homestead. Samuel Foote emerged from the house and adjusted his suspenders as Adam pulled the reins to stop the team. Barely tipping his hat, Adam said, "Morning, Foote."

"What do you want?" Foote demanded.

"Have you seen Billy? He didn't come home last night."

Foote leaned against the porch. "You're not much of

a father if you can't keep track of your own son. That's typical behaviour from a traitor's seed."

"What did you call me?" Adam growled, trying to control his temper.

"You heard me, Green. What I can't understand is, why you or anybody else would fight for the British during the revolution." Foote lit his pipe. "No wonder the United States kicked you out."

"Then why are you here? Indians killed your wife and you left the country you claim you love so much. You came to a British territory even though you hate them.

Foote grinned. "It won't be British much longer. I know it and you know it. And once again you're going to be on the losing side."

"I don't care who wins as long as my son isn't poisoned by the thinking of men like you ... and me. I would think you'd want the same for your daughter. Our children should live their lives in peace without the hatred of men like us." He took a deep breath. "Now, have you seen Billy or not?"

Foote laughed. "That was a nice speech, the kind the losing side usually recites."

"Have you seen him or not?"

Foote scowled and took a few steps toward Adam. "No, and you better keep him away from my Sarah. If I see them together again, I can't be held responsible."

Adam's eyes widened. "You harm Billy in any way and you'll answer to me!"

"Don't threaten me, you Loyalist pig!" Foote snarled, spitting at the horses' feet.

Enraged, Adam descended from the wagon.

"Stop it!" Sarah cried, running toward them, with Billy chasing her.

Furious, Foote withdrew his pistol and aimed at Billy. "You've soiled my daughter!" Adam lunged for the gun, but Foote trained it on him. "Stay where you are, Green. Get in the house, Sarah!"

Sarah began crying and dashed inside the house as Billy strode past both fathers.

"Keep that filthy son of yours away from her or I will — permanently!" Foote roared, then disappeared into his home.

Adam hesitated for a moment, then snapped the reins to pull the team away.

Foote slammed the door behind him as Sarah stood at the window weeping. "Did he touch you?" her father asked, roughly examining her arms.

"We didn't do anything!" she cried.

Foote grabbed her by the shoulders. "Don't lie

to me! You will not see that boy anymore! Do you understand?"

"I'm not a little girl!"

"Don't talk back to me!"

"I'm not my mother! I can't and won't replace her! I want a life of my own!"

Foote backhanded her across the face, sending her crashing to the floor. Sarah brushed her hair aside and felt blood trickle from her mouth.

Mortified, Foote said, "I ... I'm sorry. Please ... please forgive me." He tried to help her up, but she backed away.

When Sarah got to her feet, she looked at him stonily. "Never ..." she started to say, then ran to her room, slamming the door behind her.

Adam stopped the team of horses, applied the brake, and jumped off the wagon. "Billy!"

Farther up the well-worn road, Billy turned to confront his father. "What do you want from me?"

"For you to have a future."

Billy wiped tears away with his sleeve. "But by your rules, right?"

"When you have a home of your own with a family,

you'll understand what I'm trying to tell you," Adam said, slowly edging toward him.

"I don't need your blessing for everything I do!" Billy cried, storming off.

"Where are you going?"

"To start my life — without you!"

Adam studied the modest wedding ring on his finger. "You were only a year old when your mother died. You were her last miracle. You remind me so much of her."

Billy wheeled around. "Listen to you. It's not fair for you to say that to me. I can't take that kind of pressure ... that kind of guilt. Nobody can."

Adam sighed as he started back toward the wagon. "I'll be waiting for you at home."

"Pa?"

"Yes?"

"How did ... how did you know Ma was the one for you? How did you know you loved her?"

Adam's conflicted feelings churned inside him as he wondered whether to scold Billy for his love of Sarah or tenderly explain his son's feelings. "I didn't want her to leave. Any time I saw her I didn't want her to go ... and counted the hours until I could see her again." He smiled. "I didn't care what anybody said. I would've done anything to be with her."

"Don't I deserve the same chance?" Billy asked, eyes locked on his father.

Adam shook his head. "This is different, Billy. There's a war on, and Samuel Foote is full of hate."

"So are you."

"Yes, I am, and I pray you're never like that. But you're young still and haven't experienced life fully." Adam glanced at his ring again. "Love is hard enough without war and all the problems it brings. At least wait until we know what's going to happen. Wait until emotions aren't running so high. Wanting to marry Sarah is only making a hard situation harder — for you and for her."

"And for you and Mr. Foote, too, right?"

"Yes, and even though I don't see eye-to-eye with him, I understand his position. We're both parents and we both want what we think is best for our children. It's hypocritical I know, but that's the way it is. Someday you'll understand what I'm saying."

"What if I run away and join the army? Would you still ... you know ..."

"Love you? Of course I would. Do you really think I want to see you get hurt or killed? It would destroy me. To see a young man with so much potential, more than I ever had, throw it all away for a war nobody wants, would make my life unbearable." He placed a hand on his son's shoulder. "Billy, I know you're brave and want to fight for your country, but I need you more. Your family needs you more. Sarah will need you more if you end up together. Come home now, please."

Billy fell silent for a moment, brimming with mixed emotions. Then he reached into his pocket, withdrew the straw ring, contemplated it briefly, and tossed it into a nearby puddle. Adam tousled his son's hair, and Billy retaliated with a light punch at his father's stomach as they laughed and wrestled back to the wagon.

The brilliant sun blazed over a perfectly still Lake Ontario. The stifling heat silenced nature, except for the frequent racket of cicadas. Levi Green trudged through the brush, soaked with sweat, and slapped a mosquito from his glistening neck. "We're not going to find any Yankees hiding here, Billy."

"Then go home. I know Pa told you to follow me." Billy quickened his pace as Levi collapsed beside a creek at the edge of the escarpment and splashed water on his burning face with his hat. "I won't be coming home tonight," Billy added casually over his shoulder. "I'm joining the army."

"What? You promised Pa you wouldn't."

"I know what I told him."

Levi stood and donned his hat. "I'm supposed to look after you — and that's exactly what I intend to do!"

"Walk away, Levi. This doesn't concern you."

"I'll drag you home kicking and screaming if I have to." Before Levi could say anything more, Billy punched him in the mouth, decking him. Levi flexed his jaw with his hand as his brother stood over him, fists clenched. "Not a bad punch." He pulled himself to his feet. "Now try that when I'm ready."

Billy raised his hands and shadowed his brother. "You'll have to knock me unconscious to stop me!"

Levi grinned and rolled up his sleeves. "If you insist. It's about time somebody taught you a lesson."

They circled each other as Billy threw a few punches but missed badly. Levi lunged at him, tackling Billy to the ground, but Billy pushed his brother aside with a blow to the gut. The older brother playfully hauled Billy to his feet and placed him in a headlock, but suddenly stopped. "My God," he whispered, quickly pulling Billy to the ground in a cloud of dust.

Directly below them, at the base of the escarpment, a mile-long blue river of three thousand American soldiers marched toward Stoney Creek.

The smartly dressed U.S. Cavalry wore blue coats with silver buttons and silver braid, white buckskin pants, knee-high black boots, leather helmets wrapped with silver metal topped with white horsehair, and curved sabres at their hips. The infantry marched haphazardly, wearing blue coats and white pants, guns slung over shoulders, barrels down. Six horse teams pulled black cannons, while the mounted artillery units wore blue coats with brass buttons and gold lace. Behind them were supply wagons with Generals Winder and Chandler riding their horses side by side. After them came an ensign carrying a blue-and-white flag with fifteen stars as red-clad musicians kept time on deep, rope-bound drums along with fifers playing "Cottage in the Woods."

In all the massive American force consisted of three companies of artillery with nine field guns, two detachments of riflemen, one squadron of dragoons, and eight infantry units.

Billy and Levi exchanged shocked glances. "There must be thousands of them," Billy muttered.

"That's not a regiment — it's an army!" Levi countered under his breath.

"Let's take a closer look!" Billy suggested, racing off before Levi could stop him.

The tail end of the American column struggled to march in the sloppy muck. Soldiers fought to lift their legs with each step as the foot-deep mud sucked their boots off. Several men slipped and fell head first into the sludge, but nobody laughed as the searing sun drained everyone's energy.

At the rear soldiers tried to heave a string of artillery and wagons trapped in the mud. Another group strained to lug heavy tree trunks strewn across the path as Chandler and Winder watched atop their horses.

"You're all unfit to wear the uniform of the United States Army!" Winder shouted.

"That will be enough!" Chandler snapped, wiping his sweaty face with a forearm.

"If our men can't even remove the enemy's barricades in retreat, how will they fight when we find them?"

"I don't think our soldiers' abilities are in question, but perhaps yours are." Chandler turned to a nearby brigade grappling with a huge tree trunk. "Good work, gentlemen!"

One soldier laboured to pry a wagon wheel from the ooze, but suddenly noticed something far off. He squinted to see better and then a look of terror disfigured his face. Before he could say anything an arrow sliced through his chest, causing him to step back awkwardly and fall dead. The other troops immediately dropped what they were doing and scrambled to take up arms and fire blindly in all directions.

At the top of a hill John Norton signalled his band of Indians to fire their muskets continuously while others launched arrows. Several American soldiers were instantly killed as the wounded shrieked in agony trying to remove lethal missiles from their limbs.

Chandler's and Winder's horses bucked at the cacophony as both fought to maintain their mounts. "I suggest we send our sharpshooters!" Winder cried.

"No!" Chandler said. "We can't spare anyone. Besides, the Indians are too experienced in guerrilla warfare."

"They've harassed us ever since we left Fort George! Do *something*!"

"I'm in command, Mr. Winder. We're going to need all the manpower we can get to fight at Burlington Heights. Take the point."

Winder spat and rode off. "Incompetent idiot! He's going to get us all killed!"

At the base of the escarpment, hidden by the dense brush, Billy and Levi watched as the last of the American line marched off.

"We have to warn everybody," Billy whispered.

"Let's have a little fun first," Levi suggested, picking up a stick.

"What?" Billy asked, but Levi was already gone. Billy focused on a lone infantryman sitting on a log. The soldier removed his boot and winced at the sight of an open blister on his foot. He wrapped the injury with a piece of cloth just as Levi stealthily came up behind him and whacked him across the backside. The soldier let out a loud yelp before falling face first into the mud as Levi vanished into the woodland.

At the vanguard of the American forces the Indian assault was finished. Winder surveyed the dozens of casualties as the able-bodied began digging graves and provided medical aid. One frightened teenage soldier knelt beside a tree with his head in his hands and sobbed uncontrollably.

Winder dismounted and dragged the youngster to his feet before slamming him against a tree. "Pull yourself together, man! The callow soldier wept even harder as Winder angrily drew his pistol. "Coward! Stop it!"

The soldier slowly raised a trembling hand and pointed at a deceased infantryman, the body still standing, arrows pinning it to a wagon. The crying soldier sank into Winder's arms. "He's my brother."

Winder's face softened as he held the boy tightly. "It's okay, son. You're going to fight and avenge your brother's death."

"I ... I can't ... go on, sir."

"Get on your feet, or I'll slay you right here!" Winder suddenly shouted, then yanked the young man to his feet. The general gestured to a group of other men. "I want you to move on ahead and confine the settlers to their homes. I don't want any of them to warn the British at Burlington Heights. And take whatever food and ammunition you can find."

As Billy and Levi scrambled back up the escarpment, an American soldier fired his musket at them. The bullet whizzed over their heads, and they laughed as they swiftly climbed out of range. While they ran, Billy glanced at his brother. "I think I can forget about joining the army. From here on we're all soldiers."

"We should split up and warn as many people as we can," Levi said, winking. "See you soon." He bolted toward a patch of evergreens.

"Levi?" Billy cried, and Levi stopped. "Were you really going to stop me from joining the army?"

Levi grinned. "No, but be careful." Then he disappeared.

"You, too," Billy said as he headed in the other direction.

CHAPTER FOUR

Breathless, Billy raced through the bush and halted at the base of the lane leading to the Foote farm. His father's voice echoed through his head — thoughts of right and wrong, opinions about their romantic relationship. Was warning Sarah the wise thing to do? How would her father react? Billy's dilemma caused him to turn back, but then he stopped and headed for the house again. "Sarah!" he shouted.

Sarah appeared on the porch of her house. "Turn back, Billy!"

They met in the middle of the path and embraced. "The Americans are coming," he said, then kissed her as he brushed aside her hair. "Leave with me now."

"Our troops are here!" she cried excitedly, looking over her shoulder.

"What do you mean, *our* troops?"

"Surrender, Billy. I don't want you to get hurt." She tried to pull him toward the house. "We can be together if you surrender."

Confused, Billy moved away from her. "I can't do that. Why can't you just come with me?"

"My father needs me. I can make him understand about us, but you have to give this up. We ... the Americans are going to take over. It's better that you accept that and co-operate." She caressed his face just as her father and several U.S. soldiers emerged from around the corner of the house. "Billy, please, listen to me!"

"I'm sorry, Sarah." Billy dashed for the shelter of the trees as the soldiers took aim and fired. He ducked as the musket balls pierced the air, ricocheting off the trees and earth as he jumped over a ridge. Sarah screamed when Billy tumbled down the steep embankment and finally came to rest, bruised and dazed. He gathered his senses and painfully heaved himself up.

Samuel Foote and the soldiers rapidly descended the hill, unaware Billy was only a few yards away. Foote stopped and held up his hand to halt the others before taking a few guarded steps. His eyes searched the area and found Billy staring back, cowering behind a fallen log. Foote loaded his pistol as Billy watched in horror. Sarah's father took deliberate aim but then slowly lowered the weapon.

"It was just a rabbit," he told the soldiers. The Americans started back as Foote moved closer to Billy. "We're even now," he muttered at Billy, tucking the pistol inside his pants. "Next time I'll fire."

In disbelief Billy watched as Foote scuttled off to join the soldiers. "Sarah ... oh, Sarah, what are we going to do?" he whispered to himself.

Isaac Corman sat at his kitchen table inspecting his rifle. His pretty blond wife, Keziah, looked on anxiously. "We don't even know if the Americans are coming to Stoney Creek," she said nervously as her husband frowned at her. "You were wounded once. Next time you might not be so lucky."

Isaac chuckled. "I'm a patriot, not a coward."

"Nobody has ever questioned your courage, just you."

His grin vanished. "What's that supposed to mean?"

She kissed him on the forehead. "Let others fight. You've done your duty."

"One battle doesn't make a man, Keziah." He began polishing the musket with a rag.

Keziah sat across from him and took his hands. "You promised me you wouldn't fight again after Queenston Heights." She tenderly stroked his fingers. "I want you to keep that promise."

"Fort George has fallen. Do you understand what that means, Keziah? The British Army will need all the men they can get just to keep this country free. If the Yankees get any farther, the whole war is lost. I have to fight." He caressed her face, but Keziah moved away from him and folded her arms. "I'm leaving tonight," he told her, setting the gun aside. Isaac started for the door and waited for her response, but none came. He sighed. "I have work to finish."

Keziah threw her arms up in frustration. "That's it? Proclaim you're going to fight and walk away?"

"What would you like me to do? Do you think this is easy for me?"

"What am *I* supposed to do? Wait until I hear you were killed and then move on with my life? I know so many women like that. I don't want to be one of them. They change ... they have no soul left. You can see it in their eyes. They're lost ... they're dead, but still alive. I don't want to be lost like that."

Frustrated, Isaac kicked the door hard. "Just what exactly would you like me to do?"

She clenched her fists. "Stay alive. Stay with me. I have as much say in your life as you do."

"Really?"

Keziah fought back tears. "I work as hard as you do. I'm always there for you."

"And I'm not?"

"Not when you leave me to go and fight. I know

it's hard to go into battle, but it's harder still to watch the man you love go off to fight in a battle and not know what's happening." She embraced him. "Please, I'm begging you to stay."

Isaac pushed her away. "I'm not going to argue with you about this anymore. I suggest you start dinner."

"Make it yourself! Why should I cook for a dead man?" Keziah flopped into a chair as Isaac slammed the door behind him. She closed her eyes and began to weep again, but suddenly stood when she heard the sound of horses. Keziah moved to the window and spotted a contingent of American cavalry approaching the property.

Isaac was about to hammer a fence post but stopped and watched as an American officer cantered toward him. "I'm Major Thomas of the U.S. Army. Indians have been harassing us ever since we came into this wretched country, and I want to know where they're camped." The young major wiped sweat from his moustache, but Isaac ignored him and resumed working. Irritated, Thomas dismounted and spun Isaac around. "I'm speaking to you, sir! Where are the Indians?"

Swinging the hammer hard onto the post, Isaac said, "I don't know and I don't care."

Thomas withdrew his sword. "I demand an answer!"

Isaac lifted the hammer again. "It's painfully obvious your parents never taught you any manners."

"What do you do for a living, sir?"

"I'm a blacksmith, but right now I'm mending some fence posts, in case you haven't noticed."

"Is that so? Well, the last blacksmith I ran into a few miles back deliberately put the nails in too deep on my horse's feet. Would you do the same?" Thomas eyed an ox by the barn.

"No. I don't care to work on your horse or any other that belongs to the U.S. Army." Isaac continued hammering.

"What's your name?"

Isaac started to walk away. "None of your business."

"You're under arrest as a spy for the British," Thomas said, motioning to two soldiers. Isaac fought back but was soon overwhelmed. "And take that ox for slaughter," the major added.

Frantic, Keziah ran from the house toward them. "Leave him alone!"

"Go back inside, Keziah!" Isaac cried.

She tried to pull the soldiers off her husband, but Thomas shoved her to the ground, causing Isaac to struggle even more. One of the soldiers went to help her, but the officer pushed him back. "No comfort or aid to the enemy," the major said sternly.

The sympathetic Yankee stared at his superior with contempt. "Sir, I respectfully disagree with your methods."

"Then you're relieved." Thomas gestured to some other American troops. "Take this soldier into custody, as well. I won't tolerate traitors." Reluctantly, the others took their comrade's musket.

"After what you just did to my wife, when I escape, you're the first one I'm going to kill," Isaac growled at Thomas.

The major laughed and then slapped Isaac across the mouth with his glove. "I'll see you hanged from the highest tree before that happens."

Keziah watched helplessly as Isaac was taken away. "Please don't kill him."

"Stay inside, Keziah!" Isaac shouted, only to be elbowed in the stomach by Thomas.

Keziah collapsed to the ground. "Don't hurt him. Please don't hurt him."

Billy raced toward a rickety wooden building with a sign that said: BRADY'S TAVERN. He turned off the dirt path and burst through the door.

John Brady, a middle-aged, balding man wearing an apron, finished topping up a patron's beer as the customers looked on. "You're father wouldn't like you being in here, Billy. Want some water?"

The patrons laughed as Billy fought to catch his breath. "The Americans ... they're coming!"

"I think you've been out in the sun too long." Brady felt Billy's flushed forehead. "If I wasn't a good friend of your father's, I'd give you a beer."

"Listen to me! They're here in Stoney Creek!" Parched, Billy grabbed a glass of beer from a customer at the bar and downed it.

"Now just a minute, boy!" the customer cried, yanking Billy by the collar. "I sure hope you've got some money, because you owe me a drink. If you don't, I'm going to take it out of your hide."

The others roared with laughter, and some even encouraged Billy to take a swing at the enraged customer, but Brady quickly slid another beer toward the man. "It's on the house. Leave the lad alone, or you're never coming back in here." Satisfied, the man released Billy. Brady glared at Billy. "You shouldn't have done that. I won't tell your pa, but don't ever do it again."

"I'm sorry, Mr. Brady, but I was awfully thirsty. The Yankees really are coming. Really, they are."

"And that's another thing, son. You shouldn't go around making up stories like that. Folks might take you seriously and you could do some real harm." Brady gave him a glass of water. "Now drink up and get on home."

"You have to believe me," Billy said, running to a window and pointing.

Brady and the men laughed again until they heard the sound of approaching wagons and marching men. Everyone scrambled to the window to discover the point of the American army only fifty yards away. The customers talked nervously among themselves, a few even finished the remainder of their drinks, then they all scrambled out the door only to be chased and arrested after warning shots were fired into the air.

Panicked, Billy glanced around the tavern. "Is there another way out of here?"

"No," Brady said. He quickly retrieved a pistol from behind the bar and handed it to Billy. "It's not loaded, but point it at me. Tell them I'm a Loyalist and that you support the Americans. It's the only way to save yourself."

"I ... I can't," Billy said, trying to give the weapon back, but Brady forced it into his hand.

"Just do it, or they'll take you away and force you to fight," Brady said as a group of American soldiers entered the tavern, followed by an officer.

"Get ... get your hands up!" Billy shouted, and Brady complied.

"Who are you?" The U.S. officer asked suspiciously, staring at Billy.

"My name's Billy Green. I saw your army coming down the road. I'm an American sympathizer and I captured this Loyalist."

"Prove it." The officer reached for one of the bottles of liquor. "Shoot him."

Billy and Brady exchanged fearful glances, then Billy asked, "Why should I do your dirty work? I'm a citizen, not a soldier."

"You're just a boy, and what's a boy doing in a tavern?" the officer demanded, helping himself to some bread behind the bar.

"Like I told you, I saw your army coming down the road and I wanted to help." Billy edged toward the door.

"Where do you think you're going?" the officer asked as he set up some glasses.

"Home. I don't care what you do to him." Billy opened the door just as Brady charged him but was subdued.

"Yankee lover!" Brady yelled as he was pushed into a chair.

"How old are you, boy?" the officer asked.

"I'm ... I'm fourteen," Billy lied. "I know I'm too young to be in the army."

The officer smirked. "I have boys in my command from Connecticut, New York, and Pennsylvania who are younger than that. Maybe you should join us."

"I'd like to, but my father won't let me."

"Leave him be," Brady said, still constrained by a guard. "His mother died when he was a baby and his old man's dying. Billy's the only one left to take care of him. He's got no brothers or sisters."

"Didn't you just call him a Yankee lover?" the officer asked suspiciously. "Why do you care so much?"

"Billy's touched in the head," Brady whispered to the officer. "He's always coming in here and telling us how much he hates the Loyalists and the British because his pa was wounded in the revolution. I give the boy some bread when he barges in here like this with his gun. It's not even loaded."

The officer considered Brady for a moment to weigh the truth of the tavern keeper's words, then looked at Billy. "Give me that weapon, boy."

Billy decided to take on the crazy role Brady had given him. "Get back! You're a British spy! Take one step and I'll shoot you down!"

The officer held his hand out. "I said give it to me."

"Bang! You're dead!" Billy pulled the pistol's trigger, but it was indeed empty. The officer took the gun away from Billy as the other soldiers laughed. "I shot you! You're dead! Lie down!"

"Get him out of here," the officer told his men, and Billy was pushed out the door. The officer poured freely from a whiskey bottle and filled the glasses, spilling alcohol all over the bar and floor. "Help yourselves, men. Looks like this town's full of drunks and crazies." His men laughed as they served themselves drinks.

Outside, Billy peered in the window and saw Brady wink at him. Billy winked back, then sprinted away.

The waves of Lake Ontario crashed against the shore, churned the surf a deep blue, and violently rocked the moored American troop boats. A small number of U.S. infantrymen hastily set up camp beside a partly burnt hotel with a charred sign that read: THE KING'S HEAD INN. Inside, the owner, John Lottridge, huddled with his frightened wife and two children as they watched a brigade of Yankee soldiers ransack their hotel.

Major Thomas stepped in and removed his hat. He strolled behind the desk and found several muskets hidden on a shelf along with a few bottles of wine. The major grabbed one of the bottles, slumped into a nearby chair, and rested his muddy feet on the table. He pulled the cork out with his teeth and spat it across the room. After taking a heavy swig, he scraped the mud off his boots with a knife. "What do you do for a living, sir?"

"I'm ... I'm an innkeeper," Lottridge said, perplexed by the obvious.

"I wonder why you have so many weapons behind that desk." Thomas flicked a piece of mud against the wall.

"Please let my family be," Lottridge said as Thomas hurled the bottle through a window, shattering the glass. The children whimpered as Mrs. Lottridge pulled them closer. "I'm ... I'm the captain of the militia. Please, I don't want any trouble."

Thomas took a swig from another bottle of wine. "When I ask a question, I want the truth. I'm tired of hearing lies today. What can you tell me about the strength of the British position and the Indians?"

"I don't know anything about that."

Thomas chuckled and fingered the hilt of his sword. "You honestly expect me to believe that as the captain of the militia you don't know the answer to my question?"

"I know it sounds like I'm lying, but I really don't. I haven't been involved in the militia as much as I used to be. My work here has kept me away." Lottridge ran his fingers through his young daughter's hair. "My family's more important."

"Your heartfelt words don't change my mind. I strongly suggest you tell me the truth." Thomas purposely split his finger against the blade of his sword, causing it to bleed. Fascinated, he watched the tiny stream of blood curl around his finger. "Well?"

Lottridge looked at his family before taking a deep breath. "You know the British are camped at Burlington Heights. As far as their numbers are concerned, the last time I was there I saw maybe ten thousand troops." Knowing he was lying, Lottridge noted the grave concern that flashed across the faces of Thomas and his men.

Thomas smiled thinly. "Ten thousand? You wouldn't be exaggerating, would you, sir?"

"It was about a month ago. There might be more, there might be less. I know the British want to hold Burlington Heights more than they wanted to keep Fort George."

"Why?" Thomas asked, still not convinced he was hearing the truth.

"Burlington Heights is farther away and tucked inside a bay. We need the cover for defence and to hide our supply ships."

"I think you've told him more than enough," Mrs. Lottridge said to her husband sharply.

"What about the Indians?" Thomas asked.

"That I truly know nothing about. They stay with their own kind. We never know where they are or what they intend to do." Lottridge watched some of the U.S. soldiers take barrels of flour, pork, and other provisions from his storeroom.

Major Thomas studied Lottridge and his family for a few moments. "Keep them under guard," he ordered his men. "Now get them out of my sight."

Lottridge and his family were taken from the room as Thomas took another long drink from the wine bottle. "Bring the other prisoner in here." Isaac Corman was accompanied into the room and shoved hard into a chair opposite the major. "Ready to talk?"

"Your death can't come soon enough," Isaac growled. "And it will be by my hands."

Thomas laughed. "Your heroics won't do you much good with a musket ball through your head." He took a musket from a nearby soldier and loaded it. "Have you ever seen what buckshot can do to a man's face from such a short range? I'm only going to ask you one more time. Where are the Indians camped and what do you know about the British forces?"

Isaac closed his eyes. "Do what you must."

Thomas wrapped his finger around the trigger as the other soldiers recoiled, anticipating the gruesome outcome. "I can shoot you as a spy, but I'd like to know why you're being so stubborn. Is your life worth it?"

"All men from Kentucky are stubborn, just like U.S. General William Henry Harrison. As his first cousin, I'm most certain this barbaric act would anger him." Isaac hoped his connection to an American general would spare his life.

Utter amazement shot across Thomas's face. "I don't believe it. I'm the general's second cousin."

Equally impressed by the coincidence, Isaac managed to smile. "I don't think he'd approve of blood relatives like us killing each other, do you?"

Thomas raised the musket again. "How do I know you're not just saying this to save yourself?"

"Everyone from Kentucky knows General Harrison. Besides, I've never met you. How would I know you're related to him?"

Thomas lowered the weapon and offered Isaac a bottle of wine. "I apologize for the way I treated you and your wife, sir. The stress of war can make a man's temper short and his chivalry forgotten. Please forgive me. What are you doing in Canada?"

Isaac declined the drink and glanced at the setting sun. "To tell you the truth, I've had enough of war. I came here to Canada to start a new life. I'm worried about my family, sir. May I go now?"

"I guarantee you won't be harmed, but please tell me, do you know anything about the British and the Indians?"

"Nothing. Like I said, I've had enough of war and I don't want anything to do with this. I'm a simple farmer and blacksmith." Isaac offered his hand. "But good luck to you." They shook hands, then Isaac turned for the door.

"By the way, you'll need the password to get through our lines," Thomas said. "As kin, you have to promise not to give it to the enemy. Doing so would be treason."

Isaac placed his hand over his heart. "You have my word."

"It's Wil-Hen-Har," Thomas said with a grin. "Code for William Henry Harrison."

Isaac tipped his hat and walked out.

Major Thomas withdrew a half-burnt cigar, lit it, and looked at two of his men. "Follow him, but do it discreetly. In war you can't even trust family."

A tiny wisp of smoke rose straight up from the chimney of a white two-storey farmhouse. The home was nestled on a cleared area of land, surrounded by woodland and a cedar swamp on one side, and the tangled foothills of the escarpment on the other.

Inside the house a widow named Mary Gage sat at her kitchen table peeling potatoes. She smiled warmly at the painting of her late husband in the front hallway. Two other paintings showed her two grown sons. All were portraits from the waist up, indicating a certain degree of wealth. Each man held a Bible, conveying religion as the most important aspect of his life.

Suddenly, Mary thought she heard something and stopped working. After a few seconds, she began peeling again just as there was a flash by one of her windows. Carefully, she pulled the curtain aside as her door crashed open. Several U.S. soldiers stormed inside. Mary screamed and ran for another door. When she threw it open, she discovered more Yankees waiting for her.

Clambering up the stairs to the second floor, Mary bolted into a bedroom and barricaded the door behind her with a chair. She inched away and covered her mouth with trembling hands when she heard heavy footsteps coming up the staircase. Mary slid down the wall and caught a glimpse of the thousands of American soldiers converging upon her property. Her eyes widened in horror as the bedroom door was smashed open.

Downstairs, Generals Chandler and Winder scoped out the home. "We'll use this house as our headquarters until we decide when to attack Burlington Heights," Chandler said, peering out the window when he heard skittish animals. At the barn some of the American soldiers awkwardly tried to round up the nervous livestock.

Mary was escorted into the room and fretfully looked out the window where a soldier held a knife to the throat of one of her sheep. "Please, I beg you, don't hurt my animals!"

Chandler quickly swiped the curtain closed, and then they all heard the death cry of the animal. The men outside laughed, rejoicing over the fine meal they would have tonight.

Mary collapsed into a chair as Chandler placed a comforting hand on her shoulder. "I'm sorry, madam, but it's a necessity of war to feed my army."

Winder rolled his eyes and gestured to the guards. "Lock her in the fruit cellar."

"No, please don't!" Mary cried.

Chandler turned away as the widow was subdued and forced downstairs. "Was that absolutely necessary?" he asked Winder.

"What would you like me to do — let her walk away and tell the British we're here?" Winder took a bite from a peeled potato. "I realize you're in command, but if you don't have the stomach for this sort of thing, then leave it to me."

Chandler reflected for a moment, then said, "I think we should post some of the men in a square mile around this property. The British might launch an attack."

Winder eased into a chair and continued eating. "The settlers have been confined to their homes. The British don't even know we're here."

At that moment a man wearing tattered clothes and walking with a limp was brought into the room.

"What does this peasant want?" Winder demanded, eyeing the man from head to toe.

The stranger wrung his hands and looked up shyly. "Mm ... mm ... my name issss ... Fitzgibbon. I www ... would like to sss ... sell mm ... my butter to your arm ... army." He wiped drool from his mouth.

"I thought he might be a spy, sirs," an American soldier said.

Winder scowled. "Don't be so stupid, man. Take a good look at this stuttering idiot."

"I ... I just www ... want to mm ... make some mm ... money," Fitzgibbon said, coughing.

Chandler waved Fitzgibbon out. "For God's sake, let him sell his wares. We have more important things to discuss."

Fitzgibbon nodded his appreciation and tripped over a chair, causing him to fall to the floor. Embarrassed, he grinned dumbly, picked himself up, and staggered out the door.

"If all the British are as moronic as that man, hardly a shot will have to be fired," Winder said as he searched the house's cabinets.

Chandler took a seat and plunked his feet on another chair. "You may be right, Mr. Winder, you may be right."

"Lord, it does my heart good to see you finally

relax." Winder found a bottle of whiskey. He uncorked it, poured two glasses, and raised his. "To comrades in arms! To friendship!"

CHAPTER FIVE

A droplet of blood splattered on the ground as Billy flinched, pulling out the thistles in his arms and legs. He peered over the precipice of the escarpment at the Gage property below. "Poor Mrs. Gage."

The area was teeming with thousands of American soldiers busy with activity — cooks preparing the slaughtered animals and baking bread, others erecting hundreds of tents, more digging up fence posts and building fires.

Billy moved back into the safety of the forest, dodging the elms and pines and jumping over small swampy areas. Frequently, he stopped to catch his breath as his nervous eyes scanned the dense brush for signs of the enemy. He followed a ridge, descended the steep hill, then hid behind a bush where he gazed at a small house tucked amid the trees. After a couple of minutes, he ran toward the home and knocked lightly on the door.

It opened slightly to reveal Levi holding a rifle, with his wife, Tina, and their baby, Hannah, behind him. "Thank God you're okay."

"I tried to warn as many as I could," Billy said as Tina handed him a cup of cold water.

"What about Pa?" Levi asked. "And Keziah and Isaac? We have to tell them, too."

Billy downed the rest of the water. "It's too risky. The Americans are everywhere."

"They've got to be told," Levi said, slinging the musket over his shoulder.

"You heard Billy," Tina said. "There isn't time. We should hide in one of the trapping huts until it's safe to come out again."

"She's right, Levi," Billy said. "The Yanks have captured the town and are searching all the homes. It's only a matter of time before they get here."

"Please, Levi," Tina pleaded.

Her husband hesitated for a moment before quickly gathering some provisions and tossing them into a canvas bag. Then Levi and his family hurried out the door, and Billy led them along a narrow path.

"Hurry!" Billy urged. "I know the fastest way."

Tina stumbled but managed to hold on to the baby. Levi helped her up as Billy halted at the edge of the escarpment.

"The closest hut is about twenty feet down behind some fallen trees," Billy told them. He spotted several U.S. soldiers climbing toward them.

One of the troops saw Billy and fired his musket. Hannah was nearly hit as the bullet lodged itself in a tree. Tina screamed and held her baby tightly as Levi pulled them away, but Billy remained.

"Come on!" Levi shouted at Billy.

"I'll distract them," Billy said, gazing over the edge. The Yankees were only yards away.

Tina tugged at Levi's shirt until he finally disappeared with them into the brush.

Billy ran in a different direction, and the Americans followed him through the tangled vegetation. He hid behind some bushes and hollered an Indian war cry. The soldiers froze, terrified, then fired aimlessly in all directions.

"Let's get out of here!" one of the men cried, and they hastily retreated.

Relieved, Billy slumped down to catch his breath and noticed the tree beside him. Inscribed into the wood was a heart he had drawn months ago with his name and Sarah's. He ran his finger along the etching and sadly lowered his head.

Sarah Foote softly stroked one of the horse's faces as she watched her father lift several bags of flour into their wagon, followed by a barrel of pork. Finally, he added some blankets and muskets. "I'm a patriot, Sarah. I have to help. Besides, this is a great opportunity for us. Once this country has been captured — and there's no doubt that it will be — I'm sure I'll be rewarded for my assistance." Foote climbed into the wagon's seat. "One day you'll thank me for this. This is something you can proudly tell your grandchildren about."

"When Billy becomes my husband, there will be two sides to the story," Sarah said.

"As long as I'm alive, that's not going to happen. Even if I were dead, marrying that traitor would shame the family name. Remember that."

Sarah fought back tears. "Please stay. I'm scared to be alone."

He cupped her chin. "I'm ... I'm sorry about this morning. I'll never raise my hand to you again. I promise."

"What if something happens to you?" she asked, holding his hand close against her face.

Foote leaned down and kissed her forehead. "I'll be back in the morning. I'm just going to give these things to our army and find out what their plans are. You stay inside until I get back."

"I might not be here."

Foote was unsure for a moment, then laughed.

"Sarah Foote, you should have been in the theatre."

"Why don't you marry again?"

Confused by the question, Foote frowned. "Why did you ask me that?"

"Because I think your heart would soften. You need a woman to love, to make you forget, to help you move on."

"Your mother was the only woman I'll ever love. Ever."

"But if you met someone, you might not care as much about this war. Things could be different and better for you ... for all of us. And maybe you might like Billy."

Foote fought to keep his temper in check. "Some wounds never heal, Sarah. Billy and his kind don't belong with us."

"Why are they so different? They're only fighting for what they believe in just like you. We're more the same than anything."

"Americans will always fight because we're always right!" he shouted.

"Are you listening to yourself? Do you know how arrogant that is? Some folks back home think President Madison made a mistake. A lot of Americans don't think like you do. They hate war and always will."

Foote shook his head. "Those Americans are wrong and not patriots. Billy has done this to you, hasn't he? He's poisoned your mind so that you can't see things clearly."

"The only thing I see is an angry man so full of hate I don't even know him anymore." She turned toward the house.

"One day you'll understand, Sarah. Until then it's my duty to make sure you're protected from the wrong kind of thinking." He jerked the reins.

The team of horses pulled away as Sarah watched, a solitary tear rolling down her cheek. "Goodbye, Father," she whispered.

A bead of sweat rolled down Adam Green's nose as he struggled to heave a sack of flour over his shoulder. He carried it to a wagon where he stacked it with some others as Billy stormed into the barn and collapsed onto a bale of hay, completely breathless. "Where have you been all day?" Adam asked. "I need some help filling this order."

"The Americans ... they're here," Billy gasped.

Adam stopped working. "What?"

Billy fanned himself with his hat. "Levi and I saw them. The Yankees have taken over the whole town."

Adam stared at his son, then realized Billy was

telling the truth. "We'd better pack some food and hide in the woods. You get the team ready." He started to leave the barn.

"No! I have to tell Keziah and Isaac. I just came here to warn you." Billy poured some nearby water over his hot neck. "I knew you were going to town to make a delivery."

Adam reached for his musket. "Then I'll go with you."

Billy took the weapon from his father. "No, I'll do it alone. I don't want you to get hurt. You did your part during the revolution. Now let me do mine."

"We're not going to argue about this. Give me the gun."

Billy stepped back and held the musket firmly. "Listen to me for once, please."

Adam inched closer. "Give me the gun, boy!"

"I'm not a boy. I'm almost a man. I know what I'm doing and I'm doing it alone." Billy backed away. "Let me prove to you I'm a man, or I swear this is the last time you'll see me."

Adam smiled, sensing further debate was futile. "You're as stubborn as your mother ever was. If I let you do this and they catch you, this *could* be the last time I see you, anyway."

"Maybe, but at least it will be on my terms." Billy extended his hand. "Trust me, Pa."

"All right. You warn Keziah and Isaac and then come right back. Understand?" Adam shook his son's hand. As Billy ran out of the barn, his father watched him go, full of apprehension. "Good luck, son."

In front of Isaac's house an American sentry yawned, then spat at a fly on the porch railing. Inside, Keziah sat at the kitchen table, gazing woefully at the floor. A young U.S. soldier watched her with genuine concern. "Try not to worry. They won't harm your husband."

"I know you're just saying that, but thank you," she said, managing a half smile. The soldier shifted uncomfortably and was clearly weary. "Would you like to sit down?"

He tipped his hat. "I better not, ma'am."

Keziah motioned to a freshly baked pie on the windowsill. "How about something to eat?"

The soldier hungrily eyed the pie and wet his lips. "No, thank you. Like I said, I don't think I should sit down."

Keziah retrieved a plate, cut a thick slice, poured a glass of milk, and presented him with the snack. "Then you'll just have to eat standing up." The youngster glanced out the door. "An empty stomach is an empty stomach no matter who you're fighting for," she told him.

The soldier set his musket aside and feverishly began to eat.

"How old are you?" Keziah asked, returning to her chair.

"Fourteen, ma'am," he said with his mouth full.

"Where are you from?"

"Virginia."

"Family?"

"Yes, ma'am. My parents and two sisters." He washed down the last bite with the milk.

"Do you have a girlfriend?

The soldier blushed. "No, ma'am."

"A handsome lad like you?" she said, laughing slightly at his boyish charm. "Do you like being in the army?

"No, I wanted to be a lawyer, but I was conscripted. I hate the army. I hate this stupid war." He handed her the plate and glass. "Thank you for the food, ma'am."

Suddenly, there was a heavy thud, and the youth's face contorted. The Yankee drew a breath as a line of blood dribbled from his mouth. He took one step forward and collapsed into her arms, an arrow buried in his back. Horrified, Keziah gently lowered him to the floor.

Outside the house the other U.S. soldier, having heard the noise, scrambled around the corner of the home but was met with an arrow piercing his chest. He tried to remove the projectile, but then another arrow slammed into his thigh. The soldier let out a loud cry as several Indians converged upon him with their knives raised.

Inside, Keziah cradled the young soldier's head in her lap and rocked him as he quietly wept for his life. With moistened eyes she watched as he convulsed for a moment and then went limp. After a few seconds, she looked up to discover an Indian standing in the doorway. "He was just a boy!" Keziah shouted, and stood. She began pounding the Indian's chest with her fists. "He wasn't a soldier! He was just a boy!" Keziah ran out of the house where more Indians surrounded her. She fell to the ground and buried her head in her hands. Then a hand reached down and stroked her hair. When she glanced up, she saw Billy.

"It's all right, Keziah. It's all right," he said as Keziah embraced him.

"They took Isaac! They took him away!"

Billy held her tightly. "I'll find him. I promise."

At Burlington Heights a British infantryman wiped away a tear of laughter as he watched another soldier lift his mud-plastered face out of the muck. Dozens of Crown regulars toiled to create more earthworks — long, high ridges of wet soil to protect them in future battles.

Several cannons were rolled into place overlooking the water as General Vincent and Colonel Harvey strolled along to survey the work. "If they come by land and sea at the same time, we're defeated," Vincent said.

"Not if we go to them first," Harvey said, stepping over a puddle.

"This isn't the time for foolishness. Our efforts should be focused on defence — what little of it there's left."

Harvey avoided his commander's eyes. "If I may say so, sir, I think you're being too pessimistic."

"I'm being realistic. Our only hope is to resist their assault."

"Perhaps you'll change your mind when the scout parties return. Once we know where the Americans are camped, we might be able to launch a pre-emptive strike."

Vincent stopped and turned to him. "Assuming we find them, we can't spare any men to fight them."

Harvey took a long look at the soldiers working. "I think the men would rather die attacking the enemy than defending Burlington Heights. At least we'd have the element of surprise."

Vincent noticed a fresh grave and some troops digging another. "Death is death. And just as honourable under either circumstance. No, we'll stay here and defend ourselves ... and the fate of the country." He entered his tent and closed the flap behind him.

Harvey pondered whether to follow, took a deep breath, then entered.

"I don't remember inviting you in," Vincent said, surprised by the intrusion.

"I beg your pardon, sir, but I have to ask if there's even the slightest possibility we can launch a surprise attack, would you at least consider it?"

Vincent removed his jacket, settled into a chair, and studied his officer. "Do you want to die?"

"Of course not, but I'm willing to give my life to defend the Crown."

Vincent withdrew his sword and used it to dig at the mud stuck to his boots. "You're a good solider, maybe too good. Don't let your valour cloud your judgment."

Harvey stood at attention. "I'm waiting, sir."

Vincent smiled. "You really are insolent, aren't you?"

Harvey nodded. "Yes, sir, I am."

Vincent pointed a finger at his officer. "All right then. If there's a chance, I'll weigh it carefully, but be warned, Colonel, I want facts, not fiction. Is that understood?"

Harvey smiled and saluted enthusiastically. "Yes, General."

Vincent waved him out. "Now get out of here before

I change my mind." Harvey quickly exited, and the general shook his head. "Poor fool. He doesn't know the battle's been lost before it's even begun."

Isaac Corman ran along a sloppy path, following an old Indian trail leading into some underbrush. He stopped when he heard leaves rustling and waited before hooting like an owl. His anxious eyes searched in every direction but froze at the sound of an answering owl. "Billy?" he whispered.

Suddenly, a hand covered Isaac's mouth from behind as he was rapidly pulled to the ground and dragged into the bush. Isaac struggled to break free but relented when he saw it was Billy.

"How did you get away?" Billy asked, "The Yankees are everywhere."

"It was unbelievable. When they found out I was related to General Harrison, they let me go. How is Keziah?"

"Scared, but she's all right." Billy offered him a deerskin full of water.

After taking a long drink, Isaac shook his head. "I never actually believed this would happen. It's the beginning of the end for the country."

Billy tucked away the deerskin. "Someone should go to Burlington Heights and warn the British Army."

Isaac studied him for a moment and then realized the implication. "No, Billy! I saw their forces at the lake. They're shipping in supplies and probably more men. It's an invasion. The whole town's surrounded. Nobody could get through their lines."

"I can do it. I'll go back to Levi's house and get his horse. They can't catch me if I stay off the trails." Billy gripped his musket and started off.

"Billy, wait. I know I can't talk you out of it, so I might as well tell you I have the American password."

Billy twisted beneath the heavy vegetation to face him. "What is it?"

Isaac stared at the ground. "I gave my word as a gentleman that I wouldn't tell."

"Your loyalty lies with this country. For God's sake, you have the wound to prove it." Billy pointed at Isaac's scar.

He pushed Billy's hand away. "I promised I wouldn't tell the British."

Billy broke into a mischievous grin. "I'm not British. I'm Canadian."

"Look, Billy, the trip to Burlington Heights will take hours. It's not worth risking your life." Isaac looked skyward. "Besides, it'll be dark soon.

Billy shook Isaac by the collar. "Give me the password!"

"You don't understand. Of course, my patriotism lies with the British, but if I tell you, members of my own kin might get killed." Isaac straightened his shirt. "And if you're caught, they'll know who gave the password to you and we'll both be hanged for treason."

"If I'm caught, I'd rather die first than give it to them. Please, Isaac, what is it? I'm begging you. For the sake of our families and our country, what is it?"

"Wil-Hen-Har," Isaac muttered. "Please be careful."

Billy slapped him on the back and scrambled off but promptly halted and glanced at him. "If something happens to me, tell Sarah that I love her."

Isaac nodded as Billy quickly faded into the bush just as a contingent of American soldiers discovered Isaac and aimed their weapons.

"Major Thomas had second thoughts," one of the Yankee soldiers said. "Despite the fact that you're a relative of General Harrison, he wants us to escort you home and keep you there."

"Fine, but we'd better hurry," Isaac said with a knowing smile. "When it gets dark, that's when the Indians like to hunt."

Completely terrified, the soldiers followed him, their eyes searching frantically for Natives in the trees.

CHAPTER SIX

The sun set slowly, casting an orange glow across the western horizon. Low, dark clouds portended a menacing storm. Billy ran along the rough terrain and crouched when he heard voices. He parted some branches and saw a handful of U.S. soldiers talking at the outskirts of the Gage encampment. Glancing down at his chest, he saw his shirt flutter with each heavy beat of his quickening heart. Billy swallowed hard and turned for the main road. After a short distance, he stopped and withdrew a piece of beef jerky. Taking a moment to rest and eat, he peered through the trees and discovered another enemy regiment several hundred yards away. The small battery of men was marching in his direction but was unaware of his presence.

Thoroughly panicked, Billy looked around for another route to escape but saw none. "The password ... the password," he whispered to himself, trying to remember it. He noticed the jerky in his hand, quickly pulled his coat over his head, and dropped to all fours.

One of the soldiers squinted and spied Billy hobbling

across the road, remarkably resembling a bruin. "Bear!" the Yankee shouted, raising his musket. "Slow your step!" he said to the others as Billy disappeared into the woods.

Minutes later Billy scurried up a steep embankment and hid behind a tree. He scanned Levi's home. The only sign of life was the curl of smoke drifting from the chimney, and two saddled horses grazing near the front of the house. The door opened, and two American soldiers stepped onto the porch, smoking cigars.

Without taking his eyes off them, Billy ran to the back of the house to the barn and noiselessly slipped inside. Levi's horse, Tip, became agitated upon his intrusion, and Billy tried to soothe him. "Easy, Tip, easy. Listen to me. I know you're a plough horse, but I need you to run faster than you've ever run before." Tip grew increasingly skittish as Billy tried to saddle him. The animal threw its weight and knocked Billy against the barn wall, causing some boards to snap.

At the front of the house the Yankees heard the commotion and raced for the barn, their pistols drawn. Billy tossed the saddle aside and launched himself onto Tip's back. He kicked his heels hard into the stallion's side as the horse lunged forward and out of the barn.

One of the soldiers took aim, but Billy steered Tip directly into his path, knocking the enemy off balance. The second soldier fired, but Billy evaded the attack and rode off. Tip raced through the labyrinth of low branches as Billy ducked and dug his heels harder into the beast's flesh.

The Americans were rapidly catching up as Tip galloped along the twisting path. The animal's nostrils flared as it tried to maintain the breakneck pace. Billy leaned down and wrapped his arms around the horse's neck. "Come on, boy. Come on." He turned to look behind him and heard the sound of a sword being withdrawn.

Billy grabbed a low branch and released it, causing it to swing violently backward into the face of one soldier, sending him reeling to the ground. The second soldier's animal suddenly stopped, trying to avoid the fallen man, and threw its rider head first into a prickly bush. Billy grinned and guided Tip into the shadows of the timberland.

On the Gage property one of many campfires blazed, projecting phantom-like outlines of the nearby men as more wood was placed over the crackling flames. The American army was beginning to settle in for the night against the backdrop of twilight. Hundreds of tents had been erected, and now the soldiers casually milled around, enjoying the last scraps of their meal. The cooks continued serving the final few hungry troops while others were already preparing the long loaves of bread for the next day's breakfast.

Inside the Gage house Chandler and Winder played a game of cards by candlelight. Chandler glanced out the window with a worried look on his tired face. "This doesn't feel right. The men are too disorganized and undisciplined." He watched some of the soldiers wrestling on the ground.

"As usual you worry too much," Winder said.

"Aren't you concerned that the British might launch a night attack?"

Winder rolled his eyes and took a large bite out of a loaf of bread. "You know what you are? An alarmist. The British are hardly in a position to attack us. Besides, we haven't seen any of their scout parties. They don't even know we're here."

"Don't be so sure." Chandler bit his lip and looked up at the moon before it was covered by clouds.

Winder spread a healthy amount of butter on another piece of bread. "You know, even though you and I are of equal rank, you do know the only reason you're in command is because of General Dearborn."

Chandler turned from the window. "We've been over this. What is it you're trying to say? That I'm unfit to lead?"

"You said that, not me, but it's interesting you did." Winder drank some wine. "We shall see, won't we?"

Chandler blushed, and he quickly went to the door where he motioned to several sentries. "Tell Major Black that I want him to take eight hundred men to the lake and help safeguard the supplies coming in from Fort George."

The sentinel saluted and hurried off.

"After our victory at Burlington Heights tomorrow, I think we should press on to Kingston," Winder said as Chandler returned to the table.

"One battle at a time if you don't mind."

Winder leaned back in his creaking chair with his hands behind his head. "If we keep advancing into British territory, I wouldn't be surprised if Congress forged medals in our honour."

The thought pleased Chandler as he gazed into space. "I must admit, defeating the British at Fort George and again tomorrow will definitely boost my military standing."

Winder lit a cigar and blew a perfect smoke ring before winking. "Then listen to me, follow my lead, and we'll be the toast of Washington."

Suddenly, there was a knock at the door as Major Smith entered and saluted. He was a handsome man of thirty with curly brown hair beneath his hat. Chandler returned the salute, but Winder didn't.

"What do you want?" Winder asked, clearly irritated.

"Begging your forgiveness for the interruption, sirs, but I was ... I'm ... it's hard for me to say," Smith said anxiously.

Winder bashed his fist against the table, causing the bottle of wine to fall over. "Out with it, Major Smith!"

Smith took a few guarded steps closer. "I ... I'm worried that if the enemy were to attack this evening, we're not adequately prepared."

"Go on, Major," Chandler said as Winder exhaled with disgust.

Smith retrieved a crumpled piece of paper from his coat and placed it on the table. It was a map of the American forces scattered across the Gage property. Chandler leaned in closer, but Winder sat back, completely uninterested. "I think we should properly position our guns in a defensive manner with an established rallying point should an attack occur. As it stands now, the men are poorly organized with no centre, left, or right wings to quickly form battle lines."

"What's your opinion?" Chandler asked Winder.

Winder yawned. "It's a monumental waste of time. The men are tired. Let them rest."

"I also feel the men should sleep with their muskets tonight," Smith said. "I've taken the liberty of ordering them to load their guns with buckshot. If that's all right with you, sirs."

Winder stood, grabbed the paper, and tore it to shreds. "I'm tired of all this cowardice and lack of confidence. We're the best-equipped and best-trained army in the world."

"Sir, the men aren't lacking in courage, just simple, standard military procedure," Smith said to Winder.

Winder exploded with rage and kicked his chair aside. He slapped Smith across the face. "You snivelling rat! How dare you question my command?"

Chandler stepped between them. "No, he's questioning mine, as well he should."

Winder pointed a threatening finger at Smith. "One more stupid interruption from you or any of the other officers and you'll all be relieved of duty. Is that clear?"

"Yes, sir," Smith said unwillingly, and saluted.

Chandler escorted him to the door. "Thank you for your concern, Major. I'll take it under advisement." After Smith exited, Chandler turned to Winder. "We should do what he says."

Winder scowled. "My God, man! You're letting your imagination get the better of you. We have thirty-five hundred men." He gestured at the tents as distant thunder rumbled. "Bad weather and a three-hour march with minimal forces from Burlington Heights to our position. Trust me. The enemy's staying home tonight."

Chandler relaxed into his chair and closed his eyes.

"Perhaps you're right. Maybe exhaustion is getting the better of me."

Winder topped up Chandler's glass and slid it toward him. "I'm always right. What you need is a few more drinks and a good night's sleep. Tomorrow we'll finish them off. Once and for all."

Outside, Major Smith shook his head in disbelief as he watched Chandler and Winder drinking. "Their ignorance will be our ultimate demise," he whispered to himself. He sauntered toward some of his officers where Samuel Foote waited. The major pointed to a small knoll east of the property. "I want the entire camp moved up there, including the cannons. Have the guns charged and make sure the slow matches are lit. And remind the men to sleep with their muskets loaded."

"Did General Chandler order that, sir?" one of the officers asked incredulously.

"It's not his order. It's mine. Just do it."

The officer saluted and ran off as Foote stepped forward. "Do you think the British will attack?" he asked the major.

Smith rubbed his bloodshot eyes. "If they're worth their salt, they will."

"Bring them on!" Samuel cried, readying his musket.

"Mr. Foote, we appreciate your supplies, but this

isn't the place for a citizen." Smith motioned to another officer, who came running. "Take thirty men and occupy the church on the other side. I want three sentries posted twenty yards apart."

The officer saluted and scurried off as Foote aimed his musket at an imaginary target. "I can hit a squirrel between the eyes. You could use me."

Smith frowned at him. "Are you a God-fearing man, Mr. Foote?"

"Of course. Every patriotic American is."

Smith surveyed the disorderly soldiers clumsily preparing to move camp. "Well, if you stay, you just might meet your maker."

Foote looked at the sky and then at Smith. "You believe in God, don't you?"

The major laughed, but soon stopped. "I used to ... but what kind of God would let any of this happen?" With one hand he gestured at the cannons and the infantrymen. "This war was a bad idea from the start. Every war is. Pure madness."

Adam Green hurled a glass, and it smashed against the wall. He stood and tossed the chair he was sitting in through the window. "I told him!" he shouted, overturning the table and sending plates and cutlery crashing to the floor.

Keziah ushered Hannah into another room as Levi waited for his father's wrath to end.

Adam glared at Levi. "I asked you to look after him. How could you let him run off like that?"

"Billy's not a little boy, Pa. He's a young man and quite capable. He saved our lives."

"He's not accustomed to war, Levi," Adam shot back. He slumped against the door and gazed at the night sky. "My youngest son may be killed if he's not already dead. I know how the army works. They're going to need every man they can get to fight the Americans." He stepped onto the porch.

Levi followed him out. "You're going to have to let him be a man some time. He's nineteen, after all."

"He hasn't had a chance to grow up yet. And you let this happen." Adam punched Levi in the mouth, and he fell to the ground.

Levi got to his feet and chuckled. "You're as ill tempered as Billy is."

Adam punched him again, and Levi crashed to the dirt once more.

"I won't hit you, Pa, no matter how many times you hit me. In fact, keep doing it if it makes you feel better."

"Get up and fight like a man!"

"Are you listening to yourself? You sound like Billy. That's what he wants to do — fight like a man. I wonder where he gets that from?" Levi wiped blood from his lip.

Adam fought to control his anger. Slowly, he extended a hand and helped Levi to his feet. "I'm sorry, son. It's just that I can't stand the thought of losing Billy ... or any of my children. You try to teach your child right from wrong, to make your son into a man, a better man than yourself. But maybe I failed."

"You didn't. He wants you to be proud of him. He's got courage, Pa. Your courage. And as far as I'm concerned, that's a success." Levi smiled as Adam hugged him.

"Where is he?" Sarah Foote suddenly cried as she burst into the room.

They turned to see Sarah running toward them. "I don't know," Adam said sadly.

"He's gone to fight, hasn't he?" She collapsed to her knees and sobbed.

Adam went to her and knelt beside her. "He knows what he's doing. He'll be all right."

"What if ... what if he's hurt? What if he's killed?"

Adam caressed her hair as she buried her face in his chest. "He isn't going to die," he whispered as though to comfort himself more than her. "He'll come back to both of us." He looked at Levi, Keziah, and Hannah. "To all of us."

CHAPTER SEVEN

Billy rode through the black of night, his arms clinging tightly to Tip's neck. The animal's hooves came perilously close to the escarpment's edge as Billy's eyes searched for signs of the Americans. In the distance light radiated from the campfires at Burlington Heights just as a sudden bolt of lightning momentarily turned the countryside an incandescent white.

Following a trail down the escarpment, Billy stopped at the foot of a swamp. He dismounted and calmed Tip as the horse panted from fatigue. "Good boy, Tip. We finally made it."

Billy tied the horse to a tree before wading into the hip-deep sludge. He fought to cross the marsh and hauled himself up the slippery embankment where he saw the friendly fires of the British Army a short distance away. The white canvas shelters were arranged in neat, tight rows surrounded by militia, settler, and Indian pavilions.

Thoroughly winded, Billy hobbled onward, but then froze. He sensed someone behind him and pivoted to find a stone-faced British sentry holding a musket.

"Identify yourself!" the soldier demanded.

"My name's Billy Green. I'm a Loyalist. The Americans have invaded Stoney Creek."

The guard aimed his musket. "You're a spy."

"Please, you have to listen to me," Billy said, but the sentinel pushed the tip of the weapon against his chest.

"Don't move! One more word and I'll kill you." The sentry shoved Billy forward into a tent where Colonel Harvey sat at a table writing. "Sir, this man claims he's a Loyalist from Stoney Creek. I caught him trying to enter the camp."

Billy stepped forward. "The Yankees have taken over the Gage house. There are thousands of them."

"I know," Harvey said, continuing to write.

Billy's jaw dropped. "What?"

Fitzgibbon, dressed in full uniform, entered the tent. "I saw them," he said casually. "I sold them butter, disguised as a settler. And now you're trying to sell us a lie."

"Take him into custody," Harvey said with a careless wave of his hand. "It's obvious he's trying to trick us into attacking and then be ambushed."

Billy struggled to break free, but the sentry manhandled him away. "You have to believe me. I'm not a spy. I know the American password."

Harvey looked up from his paperwork and studied Billy. "You're lying. Get him out of here."

Billy was dragged off just as John Norton, the Indian leader, appeared outside the tent. "Let him be. I know this boy."

The moon disappeared behind some rain-filled clouds, and the wind began to pick up. Fog rolled in from Lake Ontario and crawled toward the shore, eventually engulfing Burlington Heights.

Inside Vincent's tent the general pulled on his coat. "What have we got?"

"Seven hundred of our most elite men," Colonel Harvey said, scanning a sheet of paper. "Major Pleanderleath will command the 49th Regiment, and Major Ogilvie is commanding the 8th."

Vincent buttoned his jacket. "Good, good. We'll take one cannon. Any more will slow the march. You take the point, and I'll bring up the rear."

"Yes, sir. I also think we should split our forces once we get there." Harvey placed a hand-drawn map of the Gage property on the desk. "I suggest Fitzgibbon and I follow the road in while Ogilvie attacks from the south and Pleanderleath from the north." He pointed with his finger. "Norton will lead his Indians from the high ground on the southwest corner of the farm. I've evenly split the militia between both regiments."

"I just pray to God the Americans don't attack us here while we're advancing on them," the general said, attaching his sword.

"About that, sir, I'd really like to see more men going to Stoney Creek."

"It's out of the question, Colonel. If we should fail, Burlington Heights is all that's left between this country and the Americans. We need more men here." Vincent opened a drawer in his desk, retrieved his Bible, and sat in his chair. "I need some time alone. Please leave me now. I'll be out in a minute."

Harvey saluted. "You're doing the right thing, sir."

General Vincent returned the gesture. "John?" Harvey turned. "Whatever happens, it's been an honour serving with you. I personally want to thank you for your courage and your candour."

"You're most welcome, General." Harvey smiled and then exited.

Vincent opened the Bible and closed his eyes as he murmured a prayer.

Several British soldiers were asleep in their bedrolls as condensation exhaled from their mouths with each breath. The fog crept beneath the tent as the men unconsciously pulled the covers tight.

Suddenly, a British officer threw back the flap and kicked at the soldiers' boots. "On your feet and prepare for duty! I want you outside now!" he barked, and hurried out. Soon the British regulars and militia formed ranks as the Indians did the same under John Norton.

Billy anxiously kept step with Colonel Harvey, who supervised the beehive of activity. "Please, I want to fight."

"You've done enough," Harvey said, continuing the survey of his troops.

"I need to do this, sir. Please, I'm begging you. I know this area better than anybody. I know it as well as any animal. I could be your scout."

Harvey stopped walking and confronted him. "I'm sorry, son, but leave this to the professionals." He slapped Billy on the back before striding away.

Dejected, Billy watched as the combatants assembled outside General Vincent's tent. After a few moments, the general stepped out, dressed in his crisp uniform. A hush fell over the crowd.

"Gentlemen, we're going to march the three hours to Stoney Creek and launch a surprise attack on the

Americans." The general's announcement caused an instantaneous reaction of whispers, both of support and disbelief.

Vincent inspected the musket of a nearby infantry-man. "This will be a cold-steel exercise, people. There will be no flints in the firelocks, so nobody fires prematurely." He turned to Harvey. "Colonel Harvey has convinced me that this attack is essential. If we stay here and do nothing, it will only be a matter of time before the Americans surround us. This raid truly represents Upper Canada's only hope of maintaining independence from American domination and expansion. This is a moment your children can say they witnessed ... and hopefully remember the sacrifices made to keep their future in their own hands." Vincent patted the head of a nearby infant in his mother's arms.

The general's eyes drifted off, and he frowned. "If Upper Canada falls to the United States, Lower Canada will surely follow. The destiny of a nation depends upon this fight, and though we're outnumbered three to one, we do have the advantage of surprise."

Slowly, he walked along, surveying the troops. "A victory will indelibly write your names in history. Your efforts will be as great as those of the warriors before you." He halted before a teenage drummer. "This is more than a battle about the British defending Crown territory." He turned to the Six Nations men. "This is about our Indian allies and preserving their land and identity."

The general ambled over to a militiaman, who was holding his young son's hand. "It's about maintaining the livelihoods of the settlers and securing a future for their children and grandchildren. Some of you won't return, but your noble sacrifice won't be forgotten for generations to come."

Vincent scanned the nervous faces of his army and then focused on Billy. "And, finally, we all owe a debt of gratitude to Billy Green here. He's made this assault possible by giving us the American password." The general withdrew his sword and presented it to Billy. "I'd be honoured if you'd lead us as our official scout to Stoney Creek, Billy." He handed the young man a folded British uniform.

Billy's despondent face filled with jubilation as he glanced at Harvey. The colonel nodded and smiled. Billy beamed with pride as he gladly accepted the weapon and clothing. "Yes, sir!"

Vincent climbed atop his horse and donned his hat. "Good luck, men, and may God bless you. Mr. Green, get into that uniform and lead us on."

Quickly, Billy ran behind a tent and disrobed. With quaking hands he stared at the white pants and pulled them on. He was shaking with excitement so badly he couldn't get the red coat through his arms. Colonel Harvey appeared and held the jacket as Billy slipped into it. The officer buttoned it for him and gave Billy the standard black hat. Harvey smiled. "You look like a soldier. How do you feel?"

"Happy ... and kind of scared," Billy said sheepishly. "But I won't let you down, sir."

"I know you won't, son. Come on, it's time." Harvey escorted him to the vanguard of the small army.

Billy took a deep breath and began to march as the men followed. He frequently checked over his shoulder and grinned with excitement, still amazed that he was leading the way.

Major Pleanderleath caught up to Billy. "Slow the march, son."

"If we don't hurry, daylight will break by the time we get there," Billy warned.

"Easy, lad, there will be time enough to die," the major said.

Billy gripped his sword. "Everyone thinks I'm just a boy, but I'm not afraid to die."

"I hope that's true, because tonight will surely turn you into a man," Pleanderleath said, falling back into the ranks.

CHAPTER EIGHT

Hours later the now slack, protracted, single-file column of British soldiers, Indians, and militiamen tramped silently through the timberland, their profiles moving eerily amid the heavy growth of pines. The small army came across another swampy marsh as the soldiers held their weapons over their heads in the knee-high mud.

Billy looked up as a light rain started to fall. He heard the annoying buzz of a mosquito and slapped his sweaty neck too hard.

Nearby, Major Pleanderleath watched him. "Are you all right?"

"Sure," Billy said unconvincingly.

Pleanderleath smiled knowingly. "It's normal to be frightened."

"I'm not!" Billy cried much too loudly.

Pleanderleath wrapped an arm around Billy. "You should be." A few snickers could be heard from some of the other men.

"Are ... are you scared?" Billy asked shyly.

"Of course, but those of us in the army know how

to hide it better. There isn't a man here who isn't frightened." Pleanderleath gestured at the marching troops behind them.

Billy smiled weakly. "I guess I'm a little worried."

"You'll be fine," Pleanderleath said as the men came to the foot of a swollen creek. Some complained but were soon reprimanded.

Through the trees Billy spied a church near the Gage property. "There it is," he whispered to Pleanderleath, pointing.

"Wait here!" Pleanderleath ordered, scurrying off.

After a few moments, Colonel Harvey appeared on his horse and dismounted as the other British officers gathered around. "Take your men and skirt high around their camp from the south," Harvey said to Ogilvie. "Major Pleanderleath, you attack from the north side. The general also wants some of your men to march on to the lake. The last thing we need is more Yankees joining the battle." He glanced at Billy. "Well, son, are you ready?"

Billy swallowed hard and nodded. "Yes, sir! I can handle anything."

Harvey shook his hand. "Good man."

Billy took a deep breath and moved cautiously forward, flanked by a small battalion. They moved stealthily through the woods and crouched behind some bushes. Billy peered through the branches and saw an American sentry sitting on a fallen tree trunk, his musket across his lap.

The guard heard leaves rustling and quickly grabbed his musket. The soldier aimed when he saw Billy appear from the obscurity of the forest with his hands in the air to surrender. "I'm an American sympathizer, but the British forced me to fight. I escaped and want to enlist."

"Nobody gets in without the password," the American said warily, steadying his weapon.

"It's Wil-Hen-Har," Billy said.

The enemy lowered his gun just as a British soldier emerged from the dark and bayoneted him in the chest. The young American gurgled as air escaped his trembling mouth before he slumped dead over the fallen log.

Billy was shocked by the stark reality of the extermination and continued to stare at the slain man's corpse. Colonel Harvey nudged him out of his trance and motioned for him to move along. Still mesmerized by the killing, Billy approached the second U.S. sentinel, who was sitting on a fence post. Sighting Billy, the soldier jumped to his feet and aimed his musket.

"I escaped from the British," Billy said again. "I'm an American sympathizer. I know the password. It's Wil-Hen-Har."

The guard set his musket aside, and another British infantryman impaled him with a bayonet. The Yankee doubled over and let out a cry as he slipped into death.

Twenty yards away, near the church, another American soldier heard the whimper and ran toward the British position.

Billy panicked as he watched the enemy closing in and turned to Harvey, who was hiding in the shadows. "Shoot him," he whispered.

"Just give him the password," Harvey ordered. "We can't give our position away yet."

Nervously, Billy stepped forward, but the American saw his dead comrade. As the U.S. soldier raised his musket, Billy lunged forward and snatched it with his left hand. He watched in horror as the tip of the musket's bayonet inched closer to his chest. Both men stared at each other with wide eyes until Billy managed to lift his sword with his right hand and stab the Yankee.

Terrified, Billy stepped back and watched as the enemy dropped to his knees, still clinging to Billy's legs and holding the musket. Gradually slackening, the American's body finally relented as he fell onto his back, the sword protruding with the handle clenched in Billy's hand. With his last breath the dying soldier's reflexes relaxed as his finger pulled the trigger, sending a loud blast that echoed through the night air.

Colonel Harvey advanced and angrily shook his head, realizing the element of surprise was lost. "Secure the church!" he shouted. The British charged as Billy stood there quivering, maintaining his death grip on the sword.

Fitzgibbon ran up and dragged Billy away. "Come on!"

Overwhelmed, Billy remained hypnotized by the surreal scene. "I ... I never killed a man before. He wasn't much older than me, maybe younger. He was ... he was someone's child." He looked at Fitzgibbon.

Fitzgibbon clutched Billy by the shoulders and shook him back to reality. "So are you!" He withdrew the sword from the Yankee's torso and pressed it into Billy's hand. "We have to go!" Fitzgibbon pulled him away as Billy rigidly glanced over his shoulder at the dead American.

Just then a British soldier laughed as he raced alongside Billy. "Welcome to the war, boy!" he cried, running farther ahead.

Inside the church, pandemonium reigned as the Americans awakened. Many scrambled for their guns and clumsily began the loading process, still half asleep and undressed.

One U.S. officer clambered to the front of the room, frantically waving his arms in the air. "Quiet! There's no reason to panic!" he shouted over the din as the flustered men gradually calmed down. "It was just a bolt of lightning."

As he said that, the door was kicked open and several British infantrymen entered and fired their muskets. The Americans were felled as those still in their bedrolls immediately surrendered.

Outside the Gage house the American divisions were in total disarray as a frenzy of activity ensued. The officers argued fiercely about what action to take as some dismissed the reverberation as a clap of thunder.

Inside one tent Major Smith hastily pulled on his boots and threw on his jacket. He ran outside and waved to his men. "We're under attack! Form ranks!"

One of Smith's officers strolled toward him with a smirk. "It was just thunder, Major."

Smith seized him by the collar and yanked him closer. "I said form ranks, you idiot."

The junior officer grinned and shook his head. "You're making a mistake, sir." As he said that, a musket ball pierced the muggy air and penetrated his back with a sickening thud. The officer dropped to one knee, a look of surprise on his face.

Smith tried to lift the man, but the dead officer's weight forced him to drop the body. "Bloody fool!"

In the Gage house General Chandler stood at the window gazing out, then glanced at Winder, who stared into space. "Our arrogance has brought us this mayhem!" Chandler said, hastening to get dressed.

"How could you let this happen?" Winder asked, thoroughly astonished.

Chandler froze when he heard his colleague's words, then pointed at the door. "Get to the cannons! And may God have mercy on you ... on all of us."

Outside, Fitzgibbon led the procession toward the American campsite. Many of the British soldiers were already bragging about their imminent victory

Billy proudly slashed his sword in the air when he noticed the abandoned campfires. "They've already retreated!"

"Enough!" Fitzgibbon yelled. "The battle's just begun. Now fix your flints."

Suddenly, Billy stopped running and looked around to discover that the Americans had moved their position away from the Gage home to the top of a hill. "Oh, my God," he whispered when he heard the call of a bugle to summon the U.S. Cavalry.

"Fire!" an American officer shouted. The Yankee forces commenced a maelstrom of bullets and cannonballs.

The British were bombarded, many still trying to load their muskets. Instantly, dozens of redcoats dropped dead as the scent of gunpowder filled the air. Many writhed on the ground, severely wounded as the cannons initiated another barrage. The artillery blasted through the British ranks, killing and mutilating additional men.

For Billy time seemed to stand still as his unbelieving eyes scanned the British infantrymen screaming in anguish as one after another fell with each brilliant flash of musket fire.

U.S. Major Smith held his sword high. "Charge!" he screamed as the Americans descended the hill toward the field and fired their weapons.

Many British regulars were gunned down in the confusion as hand-to-hand combat ensued through the acrid smoke of the battlefield. Billy heard an officer yell to retreat, and he ran for the safety of the trees.

Atop the escarpment, Adam, Sarah, and several other settlers listened to and watched the battle below — orange flashes from the flints, bodies fighting and falling in the patchy shadows, thick smoke billowing skyward, shrieks of perishing men.

Sarah trembled and darted toward the edge of the escarpment. "Father! Billy!"

Adam scrambled to restrain her, but she struggled to break free. Finally, she sank to the ground, and he placed her head against his chest.

"Let me go, please," Sarah whimpered. "I don't want to live without them." She couldn't take her eyes off the carnage below until Adam forced her face away.

He closed his eyes, trying to block out the horrible sounds emanating from below. "Hang on to me, Sarah. Just hang on."

But Sarah escaped his grip and ran off.

"Sarah!" he shouted after her, then turned his attention back to the raging battle. "Billy ... Billy," he whispered woefully.

From his horse Colonel Harvey sombrely surveyed the morbid tableau: hundreds of dying men from both sides, some wandering aimlessly with detached limbs, while others shouted to reform the lines. He glanced at General Vincent, who rode up beside him. "I estimate we've lost several hundred men, sir." He bowed his head. "Perhaps you were right. This attack was ill-advised."

"This isn't the time for doubt, Colonel," Vincent said. "Regroup the men and prepare for a second assault."

"I earnestly believe we should retreat, General."

The general snatched him by the arm. "Listen to me. You were right to attack. The battle isn't over yet." Just then a bullet whistled through the air as Vincent's horse bucked wildly. The general was tossed violently from his animal, smashing his head against the ground.

Quickly, Harvey dismounted and knelt beside Vincent. The general's eyes were closed as blood began to puddle beneath his head. Harvey rose slowly to his feet with a renewed vigour on his face and withdrew his sword. "Regroup and prepare arms!" he shouted.

Away from the battle on another ridge, John Norton and his tribal allies watched the fray. "The British are losing. This is a pointless slaughter," one of the Indians said.

Norton proceeded to load his musket. "We're going into this battle."

"And die with them?" the brave asked.

"If the Americans win and we don't fight, we'll be dead, anyway," Norton said, raising the musket above his head to signal the others. In an instant all of the Indians descended the hill, whooping and firing their muskets at the surprised and terrified Americans. Some of the enemy were killed outright, some returned fire, and others retreated for the safety of the woods.

Outside the Gage house, Winder and Chandler ran toward their cannons a hundred yards away. "We must escape!" Winder pleaded.

"You wanted a battle," Chandler said. "Now you have it. We'll split up and command the men."

A musket ball ricocheted off the ground and struck the back of Chandler's head, knocking him to the ground. Winder went to his aid and dragged him toward their field artillery. Suddenly, Winder realized he was at the feet of several British infantrymen training their muskets on him. "I surrender, gentlemen." The sheepish general handed his sword to one of the enemy.

Major Pleanderleath and his depleted platoon huddled beneath some trees. Downcast, they witnessed the last of the British troops on the field fighting to save their lives among the haze and chaos of battle. Musket fire came from all directions as both British and American soldiers fired indiscriminately, even accidentally killing their own men. The major pointed at the U.S. cannons on the knoll. "We must split the American ranks!" he shouted at the thirty men left in his charge.

"Sir, it's suicide!" came the reply.

Pleanderleath loaded his musket. "It's our only chance. Prepare arms." The major waved the men along, and the small battalion sprang from the forest and charged the enemy stronghold.

U.S. Major Smith and Samuel Foote watched in disbelief as Pleanderleath and his company stormed toward them. "They're courageous men," Smith said sadly, turning to his cannons. "Fire!" he cried.

The artillery blasted as the American muskets followed with an eruption of gunfire. Many of Pleanderleath's men fell dead and injured, but the army surged onward, yelling, "God Save the King!" The British smashed through the U.S. ranks and bayoneted the artillerymen.

Foote reloaded his musket. "Kill them!" he cried, running toward the enemy, but a bullet struck his throat and he stumbled backward to the ground.

The U.S. Cavalry galloped down the hill where they were systematically slain as even some American infantrymen were trampled.

The British now controlled the field pieces. Major Pleanderleath pointed at the enemy. "Turn their own cannons on them!" he bellowed.

His soldiers swung the heavy artillery and fired upon the Yankees. The ordnance literally blew the Americans off their feet. Valiantly, the remaining U.S. troops countered Pleanderleath's attack, but another artillery round ripped through their ranks. The British then dropped to one knee and commenced another fusillade from their muskets as the last of the Americans were collectively killed.

Major Smith turned to one of his officers. "The tide has turned. We must retreat."

"But, sir!" the officer said.

"Do it! There will be more British reinforcements on the way."

At that moment John Norton and the Indians converged on them. Many more Americans were annihilated as Smith bravely withdrew his sword, primed for hand-to-hand combat.

To the north of the battlefield, five hundred additional U.S. troops approached Colonel Harvey and his battalion. "Form the ranks!" the colonel shouted from atop his horse.

The British formed a semicircle as Billy grabbed a musket from a nearby dead soldier. His hands trembled as he quickly emptied the powder into the barrel, followed by the wad and the ball.

Harvey swivelled in the saddle as he sized up the upcoming battle and raised his sword. "Wait for my signal!"

Billy looked to his left and found the enemy looming ever closer amid the smoke. He glanced to the right and spotted another wall of bluecoats converging.

Harvey dropped his sword as a visual command. "Fire at will!"

A colossal discharge of British muskets ripped apart the first line of Yankees as their comrades behind them returned the salvo. The perimeter of the British forces was decimated as Harvey watched. "My God," he whispered, recognizing Billy's face, the boy's eyes closed and half covered by a dead soldier. "Oh, no," he said sadly, then returned his attention to the fight. "Fire!" he yelled again as he struggled to remain on his terrified horse.

Once more the American lines were ravaged. The British launched another volley of cannonballs from behind and destroyed the Americans' flank.

Harvey looked eastward and saw the sun begin to rise. "Sound the retreat! If the Americans see how truly outnumbered we are, they'll surely kill us all," he told one of his officers. Then he surveyed Billy's lifeless body. "I'm sorry, son. I'm so sorry."

CHAPTER NINE

The smoky pitch of the pockmarked battlefield was hauntingly silent, save for the frequent whimpers of the numerous wounded. Most of the British casualties were strewn about the smouldering cook fires in the field in front of the Gage house. Caught trying to load their weapons, many of the deceased still clung to their muskets, some with their hands still grasping powder, wads, and balls. Dead horses of the U.S. Cavalry attracted the buzzing of flies, and a few moaned, still breathing.

At the knoll where the Americans had set up their cannons soldiers from both sides lay sprawled over the guns. British and American infantrymen lay side by side, maintaining their last pose of combat. Fatal musket wounds were evident for most of the British, and the dead U.S. troops revealed gaping bayonet injuries. Crushed tents and supplies littered the battlefield as birds descended to reap the harvest.

The outline of an American horseman was barely

visible through the haze as he rode to the centre of the war zone. In his hand was a flag of truce, flapping in the breeze. He met a British counterpart and saluted. The Crown officer returned the salutation.

"Sir, we respectfully request a ceasefire to retrieve our dead and wounded," the American said.

The British officer nodded his approval, and both turned and rode off in separate directions.

A few hundred yards away in a tent by the knoll a U.S. Cavalry colonel named James Burn stood nervously before a handful of other officers and scratched his head. "I ... I must assume command, gentlemen. I guess I'm the only senior officer left. I just don't know whether we should stand firm or counterattack."

"We should counterattack immediately!" Major Thomas said, angrily kicking aside a chair. "I say the battle was even. Now we should finish it."

Major Smith took a seat, completely exhausted. "For all we know there are Indians in the woods and possibly more British reinforcements on the way. Half our men ran into the woods. We should get away while we can."

"And just leave everything?" Thomas asked.

"We'll burn our supplies and baggage so the British can't use them. Our retreat must be light," Burns said, slightly more sure of himself.

"That's it?" Thomas said incredulously. "That's your answer?"

"I'm in charge now, Major," Burns snapped. "Our men are scattered all over the place and a few hundred of our men are dead. What would you like me to do? Tell your men we're leaving at noon for Fort George." He started to walk away but stopped and turned back. "And burn every building on the way, especially their stores. I want them to remember this day."

On the opposite side of the property, Colonel Harvey, Major Pleanderleath, and John Norton stared at the bloody battlefield, trying to gauge the situation through the murkiness.

Harvey looked through his field glass at the tattered American forces. "If they have any idea how outnumbered we are, this nightmare has just begun," he said as a junior officer ran toward them.

"Sirs, one of our scouts infiltrated their camp," the officer said, still trying to catch his breath. "The Americans are going to retreat."

"I believe we control the field, sir," Pleanderleath said happily.

Norton smiled. "I think I can make their retreat a

little faster. I'll have my men start shouting war cries. We can have the settlers do the same. If there's one thing the Yankees are scared of, it's Indians."

"Good idea, John," Harvey said as he climbed onto his horse. "I suggest we set up the Gage house as a hospital, Major." The colonel extended his hand. "The Crown thanks you and your men, John. I hope I'll see you again soon." Norton shook their hands and then rode off as Harvey turned to Pleanderleath. "Have some scouts follow the Americans. I want to make sure they go away for good."

"Yes, sir," Pleanderleath said, snapping a smart salute before hurrying off with the junior officer.

Harvey peered through his scope again and surveyed the field of death. Scanning along, he saw a young soldier stagger to his feet. It was Billy. "Well, I'll be."

Billy rubbed his eyes, which stung from the heavy smoke still lingering in the air. Through the fog he recoiled with revulsion at the sight of hundreds of dead bodies from both armies scattered on the rich green swath. He heard the groans of wounded and dying men as he watched the crippled being hurried away by American and British medics.

Finally, Billy managed to pull his attention away and discovered Samuel Foote contorted in pain and gasping for air. He ran to Sarah's father and knelt.

"Help me," Foote whispered. "Please ... help me."

Carefully, Billy lifted the man's head and noticed a bullet puncture in his neck. "I need a doctor! Someone get a doctor!" He looked around frantically.

"My Sarah ... promise me you'll look after her," Foote said as Billy nodded. "Tell her I'm sorry. Tell her I love her."

"I will, sir," Billy said, choking back emotion.

"I'm sorry, Billy. I haven't treated you very kindly." Foote licked his parched lips. "I hope you can forgive me."

Billy stroked the man's forehead. "There's nothing to forgive, sir."

"I never thought it would end like this. Strange how your life ends in a way you never expected. Remember that." Foote flinched from the pain. "Are you scared to die, Billy?"

Billy forced a smile. "Yes ... yes, sir, I am. But you're not going to die."

"I'm scared, too," Foote said quietly as Billy held his hand. Suddenly, Foote convulsed as his eyes rolled back with one last exhale. Billy embraced the man's lifeless body and began to weep softly.

Generals Winder and Chandler stood before a table inside a tent with several British guards behind them. General Vincent sat at the table, his head wrapped with cloth as Colonel Harvey perched in the other chair. "You disgust me, sirs," Vincent said as he wiped away a trickle of blood from beneath his bandage. "Loading your muskets with buckshot is nothing short of barbaric."

Ashamed, Chandler merely looked down, but Winder grinned. "War is war, General. One must do whatever one can to win."

"Well, you didn't win," Harvey snapped, leaning toward the two American generals. "Your forces are pretty shaken. You outnumbered us three to one, and yet it's your forces that are retreating."

"The war isn't over," Winder shot back, crossing his arms. "One insignificant battle doesn't change anything."

"As the officer in charge, I suggest you keep your arrogant mouth shut," Chandler said, glaring at Winder. "May I ask how many of our men were killed, sir?" Chandler asked Harvey.

"One hundred and sixty-eight," Harvey said after consulting a piece of paper. "Two hundred and forty wounded. One hundred and twenty-five taken prisoner, including the two of you."

"Thank you," Chandler said with a sincere smile.

"How many did you lose?" Winder asked with a smirk.

"You should know better, Mr. Winder," Vincent said. "That information isn't for enemy ears."

"What do you plan on doing with us?" Chandler asked awkwardly.

"We'll release you at some point, possibly for an exchange of our prisoners," Vincent said, sliding a glass of water toward him.

Chandler drank and nodded his appreciation. "Our wounded ... are they being cared for, sir?"

"Absolutely. You're welcome to see them any time you like," Harvey said, pushing a glass of water toward Winder, who refused with a shake of his head.

"Thank you, General, Colonel," Chandler said. "You've been most kind in our — let's say, powerless position. I believe that one day we'll resolve our differences and live peacefully." He offered his hand. Vincent and Harvey returned the gesture, but Winder refused. Then Chandler saluted, as did his counterparts, but again Winder remained defiant. "General Winder, you are an officer of the United States Army. We accept defeat gracefully. I order you to salute these men. Do it, man!"

Winder frowned and finally saluted. The American generals were then escorted out of the tent as Mary Gage appeared before them. She spat on Winder's face. "You killed my animals! You ruined my property!"

"I apologize, ma'am," Chandler said, but Winder merely laughed.

When the Americans were gone, Vincent exhaled mightily. "We lost more men than they did, didn't we?"

"Two hundred and fourteen, sir," Harvey said sadly. "And one hundred and fifty injured and fifty-five missing. But we did capture two of their guns, and they're in retreat."

Vincent lit a cigar. "I feel like a fool. A general falling off his horse in the middle of a battle ..." He laughed, as did Harvey.

"You wandered around the whole night before we found you by the lake," Harvey said, grinning.

"I think this is the first time I've laughed since this war began. We were lucky. It could've gone either way. We were lucky plain and simple."

"We won, sir. In the end that's all that counts."

Vincent hauled himself up and peered outside the tent. He focused on a pile of dead British and American soldiers being carried on a wagon pulled by oxen. "Is it?" he whispered. "The cost of war is always too high. It's a stupid game played by stupid politicians who are hundreds of miles away and oceans apart. Men treated like pawns on a chessboard for the sake of what?" He closed his eyes. "For wealth, revenge, egos?"

"One day there will be no more wars," Harvey said,

leaning back in his chair. "Sooner or later humanity will realize it solves nothing."

Vincent glanced at him over his shoulder. "That will never happen. Men are too vainglorious to ever stop. The world will always be at war. Men will always kill each other and try to justify it with lies. We all have blood on our hands, and we always will." The general walked out of the tent.

Exhausted, Harvey poured a glass from a bottle of whiskey and raised it. "Here's to hoping you're wrong, General, for the sake of my children, for everyone's children, for all of mankind." He downed the shot and sighed.

Outside, Billy and two other men finished digging a deep trench, preparing to bury the dead. Other men began dropping the bodies into the mass grave as a clergyman appeared and started praying.

Billy trembled as he gazed at the tortured and anguished faces of the dead. His eyes followed the line of soldiers until he focused on the U.S. sentry he had killed. The youth's body was about to be lifted from the cart. Billy leaned over the corpse, pushed aside the hair of the dead youngster, and then straightened his blue coat. He buttoned it and used a cloth to wipe away the half-dried blood from the soldier's face.

"I'm ... I'm sorry," Billy whispered as his voice broke. "I think we're the same age. Maybe we could've been friends if it wasn't for this war." He shut his eyes. "My mother's in heaven. She'll look after you. And I want you to know that ... well, I'm sorry." He sniffed hard and turned away so the others couldn't see his emotion. The sentry's body was then lowered into the grave, and Billy walked away briskly. "I'm going to see if I can help at the Gage house," he told the others shakily, breaking into a run.

Billy raced as fast as he could across the field, but stopped near a window at the Gage house when he heard a blood-curdling scream. He saw a surgeon about to saw off the mangled limb of a British soldier. Billy's eyes shifted to the floor and followed a thick pool of blood leading to a pile of discarded limbs stacked in a corner. There was blood everywhere — on the walls, the furniture, even splattered across the glass.

Becoming light-headed, Billy stumbled off into the bushes where he dropped to his knees and vomited violently. "Oh, God ... oh, God," he muttered as he continued to heave. Finally, he wiped his mouth clean and sat on the moist grass, trying to catch his breath.

"It wasn't what you thought it would be, was it?"

General Vincent asked, with Colonel Harvey standing beside him.

Billy picked up his sword. "No, sir. No, it wasn't."

Harvey smiled. "I'm glad you're alive, son. I was certain you were killed."

Billy handed the sword to General Vincent. "Thank you, sir. It was a real honour."

"I want you to keep it as a token of my appreciation," Vincent said. "Keep the uniform, too. You're a brave lad."

Billy eyes widened with surprise as he took the weapon in his hands and traced a finger along the length of the cold steel. "Thank you, sir."

"I hear you want to join the militia," Harvey said. "Well, a militia can't do its work without music to march by." He handed Billy the regimental drum.

Overwhelmed, Billy smiled from ear to ear. "Thank you, sir!"

Vincent and Harvey promptly took a step back and saluted him. "No, thank you, Billy Green," Vincent said. "Enjoy your freedom. You helped preserve it."

Billy's chin trembled as he raised his hand and returned the salute. Vincent and Harvey turned and walked toward their horses. "General?" Billy said. "What do you think will happen now?"

"We're going to chase them out of every square inch

of this country and right back across the border," Vincent said as he climbed onto his horse.

"Live a long and happy life, Billy," Harvey said as the officers galloped off.

Billy watched them go until they were out of sight before he anxiously studied the sword and drum. His spirits lifted, he ran off to the base of the escarpment.

CHAPTER TEN

Standing outside the Green homestead, Billy watched as the lanterns were lit. The sun was just beginning to set, casting a pale orange over the western horizon. Billy waited, holding the sword and drum. He bit his lower lip, knowing he would be chastised by his father for the role he played in the battle. Billy wondered if he should turn around and run away. He could join the army. He could travel to battles in other parts of the world. That would be exciting as opposed to the boring, day-to-day existence of a settler from Stoney Creek. He would miss his family and the woods as a second home, but life offered too much not to take chances.

Billy turned and wandered over to the flour mill. He asked himself if he could work there until he found a vocation of his own, or would he fall into the rut of the family business and toil there until he died? And what about Sarah? He loved her so much, and with her father gone, they were free to marry. Whatever Billy did, it started now.

Slowly, he walked toward the house and went up the wooden stairs, which creaked beneath his feet. He peered through the window and spied his father sitting alone at the kitchen table. Billy's trembling hand reached for the knob, and he opened the door.

Adam looked over and studied Billy's dirty uniform from head to toe. "Are you a member of the British Army now?"

"No ... they gave me the uniform. General Vincent gave me his sword and Colonel Harvey gave me the regimental drum." Billy held them up for his father to see.

"Put them down," Adam said sternly, and Billy complied. Adam stood with his hands on his hips and inched closer to his son. "I ought to tan your behind, Billy." He stared at the floor. "But Vincent and Harvey came by here a few hours ago and told me what you did. They said they were proud of you and thanked me for raising a brave son. Well, I've got news for you. I'm pretty proud of you, too." Adam embraced his son. Relieved, Billy clutched his father as Adam kissed his forehead. "The people around here don't know it yet, but you're a hero, Billy." Adam opened a cupboard, found two glasses and a bottle of wine, and happily poured.

"I thought you'd be mad at me," Billy said, accepting a glass.

"There comes a time in a father's life when he knows

his son is turning into a man. Sometimes that can be a hard thing for a father to face. You want your little boy around forever, to protect him and teach him right from wrong." Adam raised his glass. "I've been blind because of that. You're a fine young man and I love you, Billy."

Stunned at the sudden display of emotion, Billy smiled and raised his glass to toast. "I love you, too, Pa. And here's to the best father in the world."

Adam shook his head. "No, son, to you, the boy, I mean, the *man*, who saved a nation."

They clinked glasses, and Billy downed the alcohol. The liquid caused him to cough and his face reddened.

Adam laughed and poured him another. "And you thought we liked this stuff," he said as Billy took a seat. Adam sat directly beside him and wrapped his arm around him. "So tell me, what did you see? What was it like? Tell me all about it."

"Well ..." Billy said, but broke off. He began to shake as his eyes filled with tears. Soon he cried uncontrollably and trembled violently as Adam rocked him in his arms.

"What's wrong?" Adam asked as Billy wept even harder.

Billy clung to his father. "I saw so much. I was so scared. I thought I'd never see you again. I saw so many men killed. It was horrible. They were so young, and I had to kill a man. No, he was a boy, like me. Oh, God!

Once I take this uniform off, I'll never put it on again. I swear it!"

Adam hugged Billy harder and fought back his own emotions. "You're all right, son. You're safe with your father now. You're okay."

"I should've listened to you. You were right, Pa. War isn't a glamorous thing. It's something I never want to see again. I thought that's what I wanted, but I don't." He wiped away his tears.

"That's when you know you're a man, Billy. When you have to go out in the world and see things for yourself. Parents can only tell you so much and then we have to let go so you can find the truth yourself." Adam smiled. "I'd say you're a man now."

"Thanks, Pa. I'd better go see Sarah." Billy started for the door.

"I saw her before," Adam said, rising to grip his son again. "We watched the battle from the hill. I've never been so scared, thinking you were wounded or worse."

"Samuel Foote's dead," Billy said quietly. The grim news caused Adam to sit again. "I'd better go tell her."

"Do you want me to go with you?" Adam asked.

Billy turned toward him in the doorway. "No, that's part of being a man, too, isn't it?" Adam nodded. "Pa? We've got orders to fill in the morning, right?"

"We do, Billy," Adam said, smiling again.

"I'll be here," Billy said happily, then disappeared out the door.

Adam raised his glass. "I know you're anxious to see your baby again but, my sweet wife, he's going to stay for a while if that's okay with you." He sipped the wine.

Billy strode along the path leading to the Foote homestead. He peered through the darkness and spied a team of horses hitched to a wagon stacked with baggage. Billy sprinted for the door. He flung it open and moved from room to room, but Sarah was nowhere in sight.

"Sarah!" Billy shouted as he searched every corner of the home. He bolted out the door and rushed into the barn, but she wasn't there, either. "Sarah!" he cried again. Suddenly, he spotted her sitting beneath a tree by the side of the house. Slowly, Billy moved toward her and knelt in front of her.

Sarah glanced up as tears streamed down her cheeks. "I was waiting to say goodbye. He ... he's dead, isn't he?"

Billy nodded.

"He was all I had left in this world," she moaned.

"You still have me and you always will," Billy murmured, kissing her.

Sarah caressed his face. "You look so handsome in

that uniform. You know I can't stay here ..."

"Yes, you can. We can get married, and I'll work at the mill. We can get our own house."

Sarah shook her head. "This place ... the memories. No matter where you and I go I could never forget. Being with you would always remind me." She rose to her feet and started for the wagon. "It wouldn't be fair to me or you."

"I love you, Sarah. Doesn't that mean anything to you?"

"I love you, too, but right or wrong, my father died fighting for what he believed in. And now that he's gone I have to believe in it, too. I owe it to his memory."

She began to climb onto the wagon, but Billy pulled her back. "I can't believe I'll never see you again." He hugged her. "I can't believe it's ending like this. Where will you go?"

"I have family near the border. I'll stay with them until I decide what I'm going to do." She kissed him once more, then hopped into the seat. "Forgive me, Billy."

Overwhelmed, Billy stood there in complete shock. "I could come with you. We could be together. You'll change your mind after time has passed."

"I'm proud of you, Billy ... and I won't forget you," she said, commanding the team of horses away.

Billy chased after her. "Sarah! Please don't leave!" he shouted as she forced the horses to run faster. "I love you, Sarah Foote!" he cried, coming to a stop in the road.

"I loved you, too, Billy Green," she whispered with a breaking voice.

"Goodbye," Billy said quietly as he watched the wagon disappear through the dust and into the night.

EPILOGUE

The dark sky warned of the coming winter as the wind swirled autumn leaves around the steps of City Hall in Hamilton. A few horse-drawn carriages drove by in the burgeoning city. Inside the government building a gathering of talkative senior men waited before a desk.

"Grandpa, whatever happened to all those men after the War of 1812 that you told me about?" a boy asked, sitting on his grandfather's knee.

"Well, let me see. James Madison, who was the U.S. president at the time, he fled to Virginia when the British burned down the city of Washington," the old man said as the others listened intently. "They still say his decision to invade Canada was the worst blunder ever made by a president. His vice-president, George Clinton, died of a heart attack in office. He was the first to do so. And then there was William Henry Harrison. You remember him? His name was used as the password to get into the American camp that night. He was eventually elected president himself but caught a bad cold and died of pneumonia thirty days before he was supposed to take the oath. He was the first president to die in office."

"Keep going, Grandpa," the boy said as the others urged the old man to continue. "What about the American generals who were captured at Stoney Creek?"

"Well, both were exchanged for British prisoners about a year later. General John Chandler became a senator, and General William Winder was appointed to defend Washington, but the British burned it down, like I said." He thought for a moment. "John Norton, the Indian, well, he got into a duel because some young buck was making advances on his wife. John killed him and was never the same after that."

"What about the British officers?" the boy asked eagerly.

"Colonel Harvey eventually went back to Scotland, and General Vincent became ill and retired from the army. But you know the funniest part of that war? Right up until the 1850s, the Americans considered invading again."

"Why didn't they?" the boy asked.

"I guess we gave them such a good whipping the first time they didn't want to try again," the old man said with a wink.

"So we won?" the boy asked happily.

"Well, the British won militarily, but the Americans convinced the English to drop their allegiance to the Indians. After that the Americans were free to attack the Indians and steal their land. And that's exactly what they did."

"But what about Billy Green?" the boy asked. "Whatever happened to him?"

"I'm not sure," the old man said as a town official and a military attaché sat at the desk. "I heard he got married to a local girl and had a family. He might still be alive, or maybe he moved away."

After leafing through some papers, the town official lightly tapped his gavel. "Quiet, please," he said, and the room gradually fell silent. "In this the year of our Lord eighteen hundred and seventy-six, I hereby call this meeting to order." He consulted a piece of paper. "As you know, the federal government of Canada is granting pensions of twenty dollars each to the veterans of the War of 1812. When your name is called, please sign your name and payment will be issued." He waved a pencil in the air, scanned another sheet, and peered over his bifocals. "Is there a Mr. Billy Green here, please?"

There were a few awed whispers as the men looked around to discover an elderly gentleman in his eighties wearing a dark coat and hat sitting at the back of the room.

Billy got to his feet and shuffled to the front with the aid of a cane. He removed his cap, revealing thinning silver hair, but there was still a sparkle in his eyes. "I'm Billy Green," he said gruffly.

The town official studied the senior citizen before him and then checked a sheet held by the military man. "Your military action, sir?" the official asked.

Billy steadied himself with the cane, moistened his lips, and stood at attention. "I was present at the Battle of Stoney Creek on June 6, 1813. I led the British Army under General Vincent to the Gage house." Billy peered around the room. "I proudly wore the uniform of a British soldier. I saw combat ... and killed the enemy."

"That must have been a great event in your life," the military man said.

"It was the darkest, sir, and something I'd like to forget," Billy quietly replied as the others in the room stared at him in confusion.

The military attaché quickly nodded to the town official and then retrieved the money. The official gave it to Billy. "It was a pleasure to meet you, sir," he said with sincerity.

Billy shook his hand, tucked the money in his pocket with trembling hands, and moved slowly toward the exit as the men in the room stood and applauded. The little boy ran to Billy and hugged his leg, his head turned upward with a grin. Billy smiled and saluted him. The boy laughed and returned the salute.

One young man, obviously perplexed by the admiration for Billy, looked at the military attaché. "What did that man do that was so great?"

The military liaison shook his head and pointed at a map of Canada on the wall behind the desk. His finger circled Ontario. "If it wasn't for Billy Green and the others, the Province of Ontario would most likely be a part of the United States today. As a matter of fact, if Ontario had fallen to the Americans, the rest of the country probably would've been captured."

Slightly ashamed of his ignorance, the young man stood. "And all this happened in Stoney Creek?"

"Yes, it did," the military attaché said.

The young man hastily exited the building and ran into the street where he saw Billy climbing into a carriage. "Mr. Green?" he shouted.

Billy turned toward him as the youth offered his hand.

"I just wanted to say thank you for what you did." He shook Billy's hand. "You know, if I had the chance, I'd like to be in a battle like you were."

Billy thought for a moment, his cloudy eyes staring off. "I hope you never get that chance, son. I truly do." He snapped the reins smartly, and the carriage pulled away.

SELECTED READING AND WEBSITES

Books

Begamudré, Ven. *Isaac Brock: Larger Than Life*. Montreal: XYZ Publishing, 2000.

Berton, Pierre. *The Battles of the War of 1812: Adventures in Canadian History*. Calgary: Fifth House Publishers Ltd., 2006.

____. *The Death of Tecumseh: The Battles of the War of 1812*. Toronto: McClelland & Stewart, 1999.

Borneman, Walter R. *1812: The War That Forged a Nation*. Toronto: HarperCollins Canada, 2004.

Childress, Diana. *The War of 1812: Chronicle of America's Wars*. Minneapolis: Lerner Publishing Group, 2004.

Collins, Gilbert. *Guidebook to the Historic Sites of the War of 1812*. Toronto: Dundurn Press, 2006.

Crump, Jennifer. *The War of 1812 Against the States (Junior Edition): Heroes of a Great Canadian Victory*. Halifax: James Lorimer & Company Ltd., 2006.

Elliott, James. *Billy Green and the Battle of Stoney Creek*. Toronto: Hawthorn Ink, 1994.

Flint, Eric. *1812: The Rivers of War*. Riverdale, NY: Baen Books, 2006.

Fryer, Mary Beacock. *Bold, Brave, and Born to Lead: Major General Isaac Brock and the Canadas*. Toronto: Dundurn Press, 2004.

Gay, Kathlyn. *War of 1812*. Minneapolis: Lerner Publishing Group, 1995.

Gordon, Irene. *Tecumseh: Diplomat and Warrior in the War of 1812*. Halifax: James Lorimer & Company Ltd., 2009.

Gray, William. *Soldiers of the King: The Upper Canada Militia 1812–1815*. Erin, ON: Boston Mills Press, 1995.

Hickey, Donald. *Don't Give Up the Ship! Myths of the War of 1812*. Toronto: Robin Brass Studio, 2006.

Malcomson, Robert. *A Very Brilliant Affair: The Battle of Queenston Heights, 1812*. Annapolis: Naval Institute Press, 2003.

Mulhal, Jill K. *The War of 1812: Expanding and Preserving the Union*. Huntington Beach, CA: Teacher Created Materials Publishing, 2008.

Nardo, Don. *The War of 1812*. Chicago: Lucent Books, 1999.

Pitt, Steve. *To Stand and Fight Together: Richard Pierpoint and the Coloured Corps of Upper Canada*. Toronto: Dundurn Press, 2008.

Poling, Sr., Jim. *Tecumseh: Shooting Star, Crouching Panther*. Toronto: Dundurn Press, 2009.

Websites

Andrew Jackson: *www.galafilm.com/1812/e/people/jackson.html*. Read about Andrew Jackson's military career and his role in the War of 1812 before he became the seventh president of the United States.

Billy Green: *www.battlefieldhouse.ca/billy_scout.asp*. A brief history of Billy Green, including a first-hand account from "The Scout" himself.

Fort Erie: *www.niagaraparks.com/heritage/forterie.php*. Take a virtual tour and step back in time to 1812.

Fort George: *www.pc.gc.ca/lhn-nhs/on/fortgeorge/natcul/index_e.asp*. Learn about Fort George, Navy Hall, and the battles that took place at this famous site.

Fort Niagara: *http://oldfortniagara.org*. Learn about the fort and its history and find out about upcoming events and educational programs that are available.

Fort York: *www.toronto.ca/culture/museums/fort-york.htm*. Explore the history of the fort and the old military burial ground nearby.

Isaac Brock: *www.historica.ca/isaac_brock.php*. Discover the past of the "Saviour of Canada."

James Madison: *www.jmu.edu/madison/gpos225-madison2/war1812.htm*. Experience a detailed history of the fourth president of the United States, including why he declared war on the British Allies in 1812.

John Norton: *www.yourniagara.ca/pages/other/583.aspx*. Read about Six Nations chief John Norton's mysterious life and his reputation during the War of 1812.

Lundy's Lane Battlefield: *www.battleoflundyslane.com*. Relive one of the most important battles in Canada's history.

Queenston Heights Battlefield: *www.niagaraparks.com/garden/qh_park.php*. Home to one of the greatest battles of the War of 1812 and the General Brock Monument.

Stoney Creek Battlefield: *www.battlefieldhouse.ca/billy_battle.asp*. Explore the museum and park and view re-enactments of the Battle of Stoney Creek.

Tecumseh: *thecanadianencyclopedia.com/index.cfm?PgNm=TCE&Params=A1ARTA0007898*. Learn all about Shawnee war chief Tecumseh and his crucial role in the War of 1812.

The War of 1812 Website: *www.warof1812.ca*. Everything you need to know about the War of 1812, including interactive tools such as sounds clips and animated battles.

William Winder: *www.galafilm.com/1812/e/people/winder.html*. Read about U.S. General William Winder and the grave mistake he made.